MISS MATCH

**Center Point
Large Print**

**This Large Print Book carries the
Seal of Approval of N.A.V.H.**

MISS MATCH

AN ALLIE FORTUNE MYSTERY
#2

Sara Mills

CENTER POINT PUBLISHING
THORNDIKE, MAINE

This Center Point Large Print edition
is published in the year 2009 by arrangement with
Moody Publishers.

The text of this Large Print edition is unabridged.
In other aspects, this book may vary
from the original edition.
Printed in the United States of America.
Set in 16-point Times New Roman type.

ISBN: 978-1-60285-485-7

Library of Congress Cataloging-in-Publication Data

Mills, Sara, 1978-
  Miss Match : an Allie Fortune mystery / Sara Mills.
    p. cm.
  ISBN 978-1-60285-485-7 (library binding : alk. paper)
  1. Women private investigators--New York (State)--New York--Fiction.
   2. Berlin (Germany)--History--1945-1990--Fiction. 3. Large type books. I. Title.

PS3613.I5698M574 2009b
  813'.6--dc22

2009005005

Acknowledgments

I'D LIKE TO THANK my family for making my dream of writing possible. Keith, Isaiah, Laura, and Julia, I love you all. Special thanks to my mother, Pat Thomas, for being an amazing assistant/manager (depending on who you talk to). I'm blessed to have you at my side on this journey.

I'd also like to thank my editors Andy McGuire and Cheryl Dunlop. Thank you for your encouragement and the time you take to help me grow. Special thanks to my agent Steve Laube, who always has time for me when I'm on the ledge and hasn't pushed me off yet. I'd also like to thank my dear friend and critique partner Ronie Kendig who just gets me. Thanks.

Special thanks to Carol Pedersen who asked me the fateful question: "Have you ever considered writing adult fiction?" The rest is history.

Also, thank you so much to everyone who attended my book launch in Winnipeg—it was an amazing evening that I'll never forget.

Blessings.

Chapter 1

DECEMBER 1947

A CIRCLE OF LAMPLIGHT in the otherwise darkened office cast a cool glow on the letter as I wrote. The hum of cars whizzing through the night, far below my second-story office window, was the only noise I could make out. Soon waking sounds would echo through the streets of New York, but at four a.m., it was as quiet as the city ever got. I took a deep breath, picked up my pen, and signed the letter.

My name is Allie Fortune, and I'm the only female P.I.—private investigator—in New York City. I was probably also the only P.I. awake and working at this time of night. Most people would be in bed enjoying the last few hours of rest before dawn. Instead of sleeping I'd spent the quiet, still hours writing a letter, trying to find someone, searching out an investigative lead. But this time it wasn't on behalf of a client. Tonight it was my missing person. My mystery. My quest.

David Rubeneski. Up until three months ago, he'd been dead. At least that was the official statement from the War Department: missing in action and presumed dead. But I'd never presumed. Up until three months ago, I'd had no real reason not to believe the claims, but something inside me had never accepted them. And so I'd searched and written letter after letter and investigated until I'd finally found out the truth. Sources inside the FBI had confirmed it. David was alive.

Unfortunately the information I'd bartered for was incomplete; someone knew where he was, but I didn't.

As impossible as the task of locating him seemed, I wasn't about to stop looking. And so I wrote inquiries and investigated. He was alive. But I wasn't much closer to finding him.

I finished the letter and sealed the envelope, then went over to the window and peered through the blind slats at the empty street below. A small section of sidewalk was illuminated, but I saw no signs of life.

Only a few more hours until dawn. I looked over at the long leather couch where often I caught an hour or so of sleep. I knew without even bothering to try that sleep wasn't going to come. I'd recently visited the doctor to discuss my sleep problem. He'd told me it was insomnia and that there was no cure. He'd recommended sedatives; I'd refused.

I sighed and went over to the record player in the corner and turned on the music. I rarely let myself listen to it, but once in a long while I sank into the song that played the last time I'd seen him. As notes fluttered out and filled the room, I leaned against the wall. Unbidden, the memory of a smoky dance hall, the heat of hundreds of bodies, and the feel of David's jacket against my cheek returned. For a brief second I felt dizzy, as though I were really dancing with him again. I shook my head, trying to blur the memory, to fade the edges so they weren't so sharp and raw. I reached out and jerked the needle off, not caring that I may have scratched the disc, just needing it to stop. The sudden silence was jarring.

I moved back to the desk and sat down, looking for anything to distract me from my thoughts. The worst part of insomnia was the tiredness that pervaded the waking hours, but a close second was the sheer boredom of being awake when no one else was. There was only so much paperwork I could do in the middle of the night. Sometimes I longed for nothing more than another voice in the darkness, someone to talk to.

I pushed a few files to the side and laid my head on the desk. It wouldn't make up for the lost hours of sleep tonight, but a few minutes of resting my eyes would help nonetheless. I let my eyes drift shut. Blocking all further thoughts of David, I just let my mind drift.

A shrill ring penetrated my foggy brain. I lifted my head from the desk with a sigh, checked my watch, and was surprised to see that it was a few minutes past six. I must have dozed for more than an hour. Shaking my head and trying to brush off the fog of fatigue, I heard the phone ring again.

Reaching for the receiver I cleared my throat

before lifting it to my ear. "Allie Fortune here." My voice had no telltale sleep huskiness, but the person on the other end hesitated anyway.

"Allie?" Jack sounded unsure.

"Yeah, it's me. How are you, Jack?" I rubbed at my face with my free hand to wake myself up. I hadn't spoken to Jack in a few weeks, but I'd assumed that the FBI was keeping him running. Still, it was great to hear his voice.

"Busy, but not bad." There was a hesitation in his voice. "I have something, some information that I really need to run by you. Get your opinion on."

I could tell he didn't want to talk about it over the phone. "Sure, do you want to come by the office sometime today? I've got a lot going on here, but I'm free until about eight o'clock this morning."

"I'm a bit tied up at the moment. I can't get off work until this evening. Can we meet then?"

Something in his manner put me on full alert. "Today is Wednesday. You know what that means."

Jack groaned. "Dinner with your parents." He sighed. "This is important. Could you see if I can be your date for dinner tonight? I know it's last minute, but I really need to talk to you."

Asking me to call my mother and change plans for tonight was huge. For almost anyone else in the world I would have refused flat out. But this was Jack, and he wouldn't have asked if it wasn't important.

"Absolutely."

A sigh of relief whispered on the other end of the line. "Supper is at six-thirty, right?"

"On the dot."

"Can I meet you there? I'm going to have to race to make it as it is."

"Just don't tell my mother. She'd lecture you all night on the proper way to treat a lady."

He laughed. "So would mine, but this is urgent."

The man was making me very curious. "Sure. I'll meet you in the driveway at 6:25 but if you're not there by then, I'm going in without you. I won't arrive late, not even for you, Jack." I laughed and heard it echoed from the other side of the line.

"Fair enough; if I'm late, I'm on my own." He was quiet for a second. "I'll see you tonight then."

"Tonight."

I set the receiver down, and it jiggled in its cradle for a moment. I had no idea what Jack wanted to talk to me about, but I knew one thing—it was going to be an interesting night.

Chapter 2

I WAITED UNTIL nine a.m. before phoning my mother. I'd spent every Wednesday for the past seven years at my parents' house for supper. And every Wednesday, with only the rare exception, my mother had arranged for an eligible young man to be invited over for dinner as well. Seven years of awkward conversations and boring dates, and I'd never shown a flicker of interest in a single one of them. My mother was nearly overcome with frustration at her thwarted attempts to get me married off. So this whole situation would have to be handled very carefully because I didn't want my mother taking my request to bring Jack to dinner as reason to break out the wedding invitations.

I knew for sure that she approved of him, as she was the one who had arranged our initial introduction, mere hours before our work lives had intersected.

I dialed the phone, cranking out the familiar numbers with trepidation, running the thick black telephone cord through my fingers as I waited.

Three rings before she answered. "Morning, Mother."

"Alexandra?" She went silent for several seconds. I held my breath. "I hope you're not phoning to cancel for this evening." Her tone was a shade beyond clipped.

"No, Mother. I'll be there. I was just wondering if we could adjust the plans slightly."

"Change the plans? How?" She sighed loudly. "Are you going to be late? Because it's not like we ask a lot of you, one night a week is all, it's the least you could do to show up at the prescribed time—"

"No. I won't be late, I'd just like to bring a friend with me."

"A friend?" Her tone was suspicious, but I could tell that I'd piqued her curiosity.

"You remember Jack O'Connor. He's the FBI agent that you introduced me to a few months ago." I cringed. Once I'd said it, I knew she was attaching all sorts of meaning to my request. I was going to have to head her off.

"Jack O'Connor?" Silence stretched across the telephone line. I tapped my pencil against the desk, nerves making me restless. "That would be fine. I could change the plans we had for this evening to include him."

"I want to make sure that you don't get the wrong idea."

"And what idea would that be, Alexandra? You've asked to bring a friend along to dinner. How can I get the wrong idea about that?"

Her words didn't sway me. "Jack is just a friend. A colleague. We've worked together on a case, and we're friends." I knew I was repeating myself, but I couldn't seem to keep quiet. I needed to make her understand.

"Goodness, Alexandra, there's no need to get defensive. I understand. Mr. O'Connor is your friend. It's not like I'm going to have a string quartet playing *Pachelbel's Canon* when you arrive. I'm not about to hang up the phone and go unpack my grandmother's wedding veil. He's just a friend. I understand the concept."

I closed my eyes and rubbed at my temple,

feeling the beginnings of a headache. "I'm sorry, Mother. I didn't mean to sound condescending."

"Fine. Your apology is accepted. So we'll see you at six-thirty?"

I sighed. "Yes, I'll be there at six-thirty." Exactly the same time I've arrived for the past seven years. I didn't speak that part aloud, but I had to bite my tongue not to.

I hung up the phone feeling drained and just a little testy. After all that, Jack had better have something mighty important to discuss tonight.

My caseload had been full to overflowing for several months, but over the course of the day I got four of my open cases off the books and even got paid for one of them. I scratched the payment amount into my account book, filed the closed cases, and cleared off my desk. It felt good to get a few things put away and moved out of sight. At five o'clock I deposited a stack of file folders that contained open investigations onto the corner of my desk. It was work that hadn't been completed and would need to be shoved on to the next day. Then I started the ten-block walk to my apartment. I had to grab a quick shower and change of clothes before setting out for supper at my parents'.

The air outside was chilly, even for December in New York, and the sky was dark, but wrapped in my heavy grey wool trench coat, the cool damp air didn't bother me. The clack of my heels on the pavement as I strode through the darkening streets echoed in my ears. The glow of light from the streetlamps kept me from walking in the dark. I looked up and saw dark brick apartment buildings flanking the street, their square hulking forms broken by lighted apartment windows. Inside the warm, cozy apartments, families were probably going about the nightly rituals of supper and bed-time. The thought made me a little melancholy, knowing that my own apartment would be cold, dark, and empty. Suddenly glad I was going out, even to my parents' house, I accelerated my pace.

I let myself into my apartment, shut the door, and removed my coat. I didn't even wait a moment before turning on the element under the teakettle. After the click, hiss, and snap of gas igniting, the blue flame made me feel warmer almost immedi-ately.

I waited for the water to boil, made the tea, then went to have a quick shower while it steeped. In picking out clothes to wear, the main considera-tion was warmth, so I chose a charcoal wool suit, stockings, sensible shoes, and a black felted wool hat. I sipped my cup of tea and enjoyed the last few minutes of warmth before I had to go back out and face a cold subway ride and several hours of my mother's company.

I walked as quickly as I could from the subway sta-tion to my parents' house. Blowing on my gloved fingers, I'd already decided that if Jack wasn't outside when I got there I would go in without him. No way would I stand outside in the bitter cold longer than absolutely necessary.

My parents' house was imposing by almost any standard. Right on the edge of Central Park, it was a stone behemoth with large windows, pillars, and formal landscaping, made even more forbidding by winter's cold. The inside was just as impressive and just as cold. Carefully placed art, beautiful but uncomfortable furniture, and a constant hum of tension, not relaxing or homey.

The sight of Jack leaning against one of the pillars both relieved my mind and brought a smile to my face. I was bundled up and freezing, and there he stood, jacket open, no gloves, leaning back, not a care in the world. Jack was a handsome man, with dark hair and eyes and a quick smile. He often looked as though he knew something everyone else didn't and was laughing just a little to himself. I always felt better when I was with him, from the first day I'd met him. He had a solid sense of humor and the ability to laugh at himself. He also respected my skills as a detective, despite my gender, and that more than anything told me all I needed to know about him.

When he spotted me he straightened up and headed down the drive toward me.

"Why didn't you tell me that you were going to have to walk? I could have found a way to come and get you." He glared at me as though annoyed.

"I didn't walk all the way here, just from the subway station."

"Still, I would have picked you up if I'd known."

I stopped and turned to look at him, despite my burning desire to get inside. "Jack, I don't have a car. How did you think I was going to get here?"

He removed his hat and ran his fingers through his hair. He replaced the hat again and narrowed his eyes at me before answering. "I thought you would be sensible and take a taxi."

"It costs ten times as much to take a taxi, and that's if you can even find one in this weather. It was just easier."

"You're stubborn, you know that?"

I felt my eyes narrow, and I crossed my arms. "I haven't seen or heard from you in almost a month, and that's the first thing you can think of to say to me?"

He grasped my elbow and guided me up the sidewalk to the door. "Other than to tell you that you haven't changed a bit? Yeah, that's it." He grinned as he said it, and I felt the old bite of friendship and rivalry between us, but I also saw a tightness around his eyes that worried me.

"You okay?" I asked it quietly as he reached out and knocked.

"I've had better weeks." He stared straight ahead, another hint that something was wrong. I knew he had something to tell me, and I hadn't known how serious it was, but I was getting the feeling that whatever it was, it was weighing heavily on Jack.

My thoughts were interrupted when the door opened with a blast of warm air. I didn't wait, even for a second, just barreled straight in. Jack followed at a slightly more polite pace, but I noticed that he shut the door behind us without waiting for the maid who'd answered the door to do it.

I turned to the maid, a young woman I'd never seen before. She looked weary. Her pinned-up hair was slightly askew and there was a small stain on the front of her apron. From the looks of it, she'd had a hard first day. I was pretty sure it was her first day here as I'd seen the look she had in her eyes dozens of times on the faces of my mother's new employees. She was a hard woman to work for, and it showed in her constantly changing household staff.

"I'm Allie Fortune, and this is my friend Jack O'Connor. We're expected for dinner." I smiled at the woman, but she didn't respond. She had a vacant look that told me she was beyond cheering at this point. All she wanted was to go home.

"Follow me." We trailed the woman from the entryway, through the leaded glass French doors, and into the drawing room. My mother sat on the high-backed, stiff Queen Anne settee, and my father sat in the only comfortable chair in the room. He read the newspaper while my mother sipped coffee out of a china cup in silence.

She was a very attractive woman, looking closer to her forties than her fifties. Her posture, her diction, and everything else about her seemed to scream breeding and tasteful wealth. Sometimes when I considered it, I felt sorry for her. What must it be like to have a daughter like me? A female detective, unmarried, and well past marrying age. A daughter who had no interest in the things that were important to the mother. I didn't do it to spite her, or at least I hadn't in years, but I could just never mold myself into whatever it was she wanted me to be.

She turned to us as we came into the room. "Mr. O'Connor, Alexandra, it's lovely to see you both." She rose, came over, and air kissed my cheeks. I tried not to laugh at Jack's pained expression when she did the same to him.

My father grunted from behind his newspaper, but didn't say anything.

"It's good to see you again, Mrs. Fortune, Mr. Fortune." Jack removed his hat and ran his fingers through his hair. I wasn't surprised that my mother liked him, despite his career in law enforcement. Jack knew how to behave in social situations, a relaxed charm streaming out of him like moonlight. Jack's mother's family might have come from immigrant working-class roots, but his father came from old money and had generations' worth of social connections. My mother chose to remember that Jack was the son of Senator Andrew O'Connor and therefore a worthy suitor for me. Unfortunately for her, his family didn't matter to me. I'd known since the moment I'd met him that we would never be more than friends. There was no room in my heart for anyone but David. But I hadn't counted on how important Jack's friendship would eventually become to me. I really did owe my mother for this introduction.

Jack shifted his hat from hand to hand, seemingly uncomfortable at the long scrutinizing looks from both my mother and me. I grinned at his look of quiet discomfort. My mother noticed the hat in his hands.

"Oh, for pity's sake. The new maid didn't even take your coats and hats." The sigh of disgust from my mother did not bode well for the new maid.

"Never mind, Mother. I can handle it." I reached out and took Jack's hat and waited until he had removed his coat before leaving the drawing room and heading to the front closet to hang them up.

When I returned, Jack was seated on the other settee looking as uncomfortable as I'd ever seen him. When he saw me I could have sworn I saw a look of relief cross his face.

Before I could figure out what was going on, the maid entered the room again and announced that supper was ready.

My father crumpled his paper and tossed it onto the floor. Something strange was going on.

My mother set her coffee cup down on the end table and rose with the grace of a queen. "Jack, why don't you lead us into the dining room. I trust that you know the way at this point?"

Jack led the way, followed by my mother, leaving my father and me to bring up the rear. I moved closer to him, close enough to whisper in a voice that wouldn't be overheard, "What happened when I left the room?"

He looked at me over the rim of his glasses. "The question is, what did you do to get your mother this riled up? She's been on a tear since early this morning."

My eyebrow flew up. "A tear?"

"She's been muttering to herself, and she was making Jack very uncomfortable just now. And she was enjoying it. She was bordering on rude."

I shook my head. That didn't sound like her. She was never rude. Her tongue was sharp enough that a back-handed compliment from her left you breathless, but something as low as being rude to a guest, that was not her style. I had no idea what was going on, but the likelihood of a relaxing, or even a civil, family dinner was fading by the second.

Chapter 3

WE TOOK OUR seats in the dining room and made polite conversation as our plates were brought out and placed in front of us. I tried not to groan when I saw dinner. It was roast squab or, as I'd always thought of it, pigeon. I still wondered at the strange tension in the drawing room. My mother seemed off today, I couldn't put my finger on the cause, but I had a feeling of dread in the pit of my stomach. Picking up my knife and fork I started cutting into my pigeon.

I looked over to see how Jack was doing, but my gaze was caught by the fancy lace table runner. I looked closer and with bone-deep frustration understood what my mother's strange behavior was all about. I turned my head to look at her, raised my eyebrow, and glanced at the frothy length of material. It was beautiful, antique Belgian lace, and I'd seen it many times before. My mother pretended she didn't see the hot look in my eyes; instead she played hostess and chatted with Jack.

I held my breath for a moment trying to rein in my temper. I didn't want to acknowledge her bad behavior. I fought with my temper, trying to quash it and just be civil long enough to finish dinner, but anger bubbled up from my throat and I slammed my silverware down on the table before demanding, "Why are you using your grandmother's wedding veil as a tablecloth?" I knew exactly what her point was, but I found it hard to believe that she'd pull something like this in front of a guest.

She laid down her knife and fork and dabbed her mouth with a napkin before turning to me. "Well, Alexandra, since it does belong to me, I suppose I can use it for anything I'd like." She picked up her knife and fork again, cut into her dinner, and then spoke as calmly as if we were discussing the weather. "It's not like it's getting much use up in a box in the attic. And it doesn't seem that you'll be needing it anytime soon, now does it? What, with your friends and your career, I can't really see how you'd manage to find time in your busy schedule to get married at all. So I've decided that it might as well be put to good use as a tablecloth. I wouldn't want to put pressure on you to actually do your duty, get married, have a family, and stop acting like a heathen. So, I've decided to use my grandmother's wedding veil for a tablecloth."

I took a deep breath, trying to calm the roaring in my head. Even though I didn't want to know what Jack thought, I turned to him and saw his jaw hanging open. My embarrassment tripled. My father's knife and fork hung suspended in the air as he stared at my mother in shock. My mother had purposely dragged a very old, very personal argument out in public. It was unseemly and certainly unlike her. I turned to Jack, but didn't know what to say. Clearly my phone call this morning had disrupted the shaky peace my mother and I had forged.

"Could we talk about this in the kitchen, in private, please?" The words came out softly, almost as a hiss.

She never even looked at me; she just continued eating as though she hadn't thrown me in front of a train, in the presence of a guest and a friend. "We're eating, Alexandra. Whatever you have to say to me can wait."

I debated for about thirty seconds. I could sit here and try to pretend that things were fine, that nothing had happened, but I didn't see the point. I turned to Jack. He still had the look of someone shell-shocked. I stood. "It was good to see you, Dad. Mother." I looked to Jack. "Are you finished there?" I asked, pointing to his untouched meal.

He searched my face and must have seen the seething fury I was somehow keeping in check. He nodded, rose, and dropped his linen napkin down onto the table. "Thank you for dinner." He hesitated a moment as though his upbringing was warring against his burning desire to extricate himself from the awkward situation. Finally he turned, and we both made our way to the front hall. Without a word I retrieved our coats and hats, and we let ourselves out.

• • •

We sat in Jack's car, waiting for it to warm up, in silence. I had no idea what to say. There were no words. Jack cleared his throat, but nothing came out.

"That was fun, wasn't it?" The words were harsh and they rasped against my throat as they came out.

"Allie—"

"You know what, I'm hungry, I'm embarrassed, and we still haven't talked about whatever it was that you called me about this morning, so how about we pretend nothing happened and we're just two old friends going out to dinner together?"

"Are you sure? Because you have nothing to be embarrassed about."

"Yeah, I'm sure, Jack. I need to get away from here, and I need about fifteen minutes to calm down. Let's just go."

He shoved the car into reverse. "Okay, what do you want for supper then?"

"Anything but squab. How about that?"

"Done."

Chapter 4

JACK TOOK ME to our diner, a twenty-four-hour greasy spoon that was usually populated by policemen and locals. The air smelled like fried onions, burnt coffee, and cigarettes. Not odors I was usually fond of, but tonight the entire place

25

felt like home. I ordered a hamburger and French fries and tried to rid myself of the last lingering feelings of awkwardness I felt.

The server brought us each a Coke, and I relaxed against the vinyl booth seat. The diner was fairly busy, and the waitress slapped our drinks onto the table and left without another word.

Not wanting the conversation to move back onto the fiasco at my parents' I decided to take the lead. "You called this morning with something to tell me."

Jack stirred his Coke with his straw for a moment before responding. "It's a little complicated."

He looked uncomfortable, but I just held my tongue and waited for him to continue.

"Do you remember that I told you a little bit about a woman named Maggie?"

Uh-oh. I sensed that this would be a good time to tread carefully. "I remember you mentioning her." I tried to keep my tone neutral.

"I got a letter from her yesterday, delivered to my office, and I can't figure out what it means."

I choked on a sip of my Coke. "How long has it been since you've heard from her?" I was pretty sure it'd been years. From what I'd understood, they weren't in touch anymore, and not through any lack of desire on Jack's part. Hearing from her must have been quite a shock. "What do you mean you don't understand it?"

Jack undid the buttons on his double-breasted

suit coat and fished in his inside pocket. He pulled out a ragged envelope. He handed it over to me but didn't say another word. His ever-present smile was missing, and I saw something suspiciously close to pain in his eyes.

I took it from him, a feeling of dread sweeping through me. The envelope contained two tiny sheets of thin onionskin notepaper, and the words and lines were all jammed close together as though space or paper were a luxury. As I pulled the sheets out, I checked the return address and the postmark on the letter. No return address, but it had been mailed from Berlin. Maggie was an Army nurse in Germany directly after the war, tending to the survivors there, but I hadn't realized she was still there. Berlin wasn't a safe place to be these days. France, Britain, and America all had a quarter of the city and all got along fairly well, allowing traffic through their sectors, but Soviet-controlled Berlin was another matter entirely. Hostilities among the supposed Allies were crescendoing in that city.

I unfolded the letter and started to read.

Jack,
I can't imagine what you're thinking, how you feel about my request, but I can only hope that you remember the friendship we once had as fondly as I do. I know it's not fair for me to ask anything of you after all these

27

years, but I have nowhere else to turn. You're the only one I can trust.

I have to be so careful what I say in this letter if I want it to get out of Berlin and to you. Is it enough to ask you to help me? I know you have probably made a life for yourself in the years I've been away, you've probably moved on, maybe even married but I have never needed your help like I do at this moment. I have to get out and I have to bring the child with me. I'm all she has left.

Please help us Jack.
Always,
Maggie

I reread the letter again to see if I'd missed anything. I read it over a third time to see if it was some sort of coded message, but it didn't seem to mean anything more than the words on the page. The problem was that the words on the page weren't making a lot of sense. I turned to Jack.

"Who is the child? And what have you had time to think over? I thought you've been out of touch with this woman for several years?" I flipped over the pages again, read the words another time, but came up with no new information.

Jack sighed. "I have. I haven't had contact with her directly in over four years. I heard that she made it through the war from my aunt and uncle, with whom she did keep in somewhat regular contact. I have no idea what she's talking about, what danger she's referring to, or who this child is. I can only assume that it's her child and perhaps Maggie's husband is dead."

"That would fit the contents of the letter." I hurt for Jack and how it must feel to get information like this about the woman he still loved. He hadn't said it in so many words, but it didn't take a mind reader to see the pain in his eyes and in the set of his mouth. He took the letter back from me, folded it carefully, and placed it back into the envelope. "What do you think I should do?"

I didn't let myself answer right away, giving myself time to think through every response I could give, carefully, before speaking. I couldn't imagine what this must be like for him. Jack was an FBI agent, excellent at what he did, but here was a situation out of his control and beyond the scope of his power at this point. "I think you should sit tight for the moment. Let me do a little checking to see if I can find out anything about what Maggie is into." I knew that Jack had to be very careful in using his FBI connections in an overseas investigation. Especially one that would be based primarily in Berlin. The OSS—now the CIA—did not take kindly to anyone messing around on their turf, and Berlin was probably the most volatile political situation in the world at the moment.

"You think I should just sit and wait? Could

you do that if this were David?" He leaned forward, his voice intent.

"I'm not saying you should wait forever, just until you have a little more information. She didn't explain anything in that letter, and you can't jump into the unknown to go and rescue her without some sort of a clue of what's going on."

The waitress dropped our plates in front of us, slapped a bill on the table, and left. Jack shifted back in his seat. He seemed to be fighting a war inside his head, so I just waited for him to figure out what he needed to say.

"I'd like you to look into this for me." The words came out as though he had to force them one by one. "Find out what you can about Maggie." He paused. "Allie, what I'm trying to say is that I need to hire you."

Chapter 5

"NO WAY. Not a chance—" I shook my head and leaned away from him. The vinyl of the seat squeaked as I shifted.

"I understand you're busy, but there's no one I trust more. Please, find a way to do this. I need your help."

"Not a chance will I let you hire me. I'll look into this. In fact, I'll push all my other cases aside if need be, but I'll be doing it as a friend, not as someone you hired."

"I can't let you do that. I appreciate it, but this might not be some easy-to-wrap case. It could end up taking a huge amount of time and energy, and I can't ask you to do that for free."

"You're not asking. I offered. And it's the only way I'll work with you on this, so you need to accept it."

Jack closed his eyes and took a deep breath, then let it out as a sigh. "Thank you."

I took a bite of my hamburger, but the events of the evening were overwhelming and I couldn't taste anything. "Besides, it's the least I could do after what you had to endure at my parents' tonight. In fact I think one free investigation wouldn't begin to cover it." We both laughed, and it defused the tension enough to let Jack start in on his supper too.

Before he dropped me off I had Jack write down a list of every detail of personal information he knew about Maggie. Her full name, birth date, names of both her parents, when she signed up with the Army's medical corps, anything that could possibly help me with my investigation. I knew it wasn't going to be easy to find much out about a woman who hadn't lived in the US for more than five years, but I was good at digging until I found what I needed.

Margaret Katherine O'Shayne, or Maggie, was turning out to be quite a puzzle. The Army had, with much persuading, provided me with some interesting information but no current address. According to their records, Maggie had signed up to work overseas at an Army nurse's recruiting drive even before the United States had entered the war. She'd been all over. She'd seen action in France and Italy; she'd been stationed briefly in North Africa; and toward the end of the war she'd been almost in the front lines as the Allies approached Berlin. It seemed to my uneducated eye that wherever the action had been the most dangerous, she'd been there. Berlin had been the most dangerous of all. The city had been pummeled by air and by land. By the Russians, the British, and the Americans. When the Russians had rolled into the city, Berlin pretty much lay in ruins, but for whatever survivors were left, it had only been the start of a new type of devastation.

Maggie had officially resigned her Army post in 1946, but according to her file, she'd stayed on in Berlin to work at a hospital there. That was the last bit of information they had on her, and it was more than a year old, but it was somewhere to start looking. The postmark of the letter had been Berlin, so clearly she was still there. It was more just a matter of finding her and discovering what kind of trouble she was in. And of that I had no doubt. She was a woman in trouble, I was sure. A woman like Maggie did not contact the man she'd left behind to ask for help, unless the danger was extreme and imminent.

I sat at my desk with just my desk lamp for light and used a pencil to peck at the typewriter keys. Typing all of this information into a report for Jack, I knew it still wasn't the information he needed. It was a start, but it wasn't going to tell him what he was desperate to know. I'd checked with the Army about information on a marriage or a child, but they had no records of either. That didn't mean that they hadn't happened, just that the United States Army didn't know about it.

I rubbed at my forehead for a second. I needed more information, but Berlin wasn't exactly next door, and I had no contacts in that city. I was terribly afraid that Jack wouldn't be able to wait long enough for me to get him the information he needed, that he'd take off for Berlin and Maggie without having a clue what he was stepping into. In all honesty, I was almost sure that if I'd gotten a similarly vague letter from David I wouldn't have waited twenty minutes before chartering a plane to Berlin. I would have risked all kinds of danger to see him again. And I knew that if I didn't come up with some information quickly, Jack would be forced to make the same decision. I'd seen his eyes in the diner when he'd handed me the letter. I knew which way he was going to choose. It was my duty as his friend to make sure that choice wouldn't kill him.

Chapter 6

IT WAS LATE Thursday night before I could meet up with Jack again. His schedule and mine were both packed full, and the only time we were able to schedule a meeting was at close to midnight. He said he'd swing by my office as he was getting off work. It was no trouble to wait around for him as I had half a dozen reports to peck out on the typewriter and several invoices to ready for the Friday morning mail.

My wooden swivel desk chair squeaked as I took a typing break to stretch my back. I had accounting to do yet as well as filing.

Sometimes I thought longingly of how much easier it would be if I could employ a secretary to do all of that work for me, but it just wasn't feasible at this point. Besides, what would I do to occupy my time in the middle of the night?

I worked by the light of my desk lamp, doing my best to ignore the pangs of hunger that tried to distract me. I'd been tailing someone for a client all afternoon and evening and hadn't had time to grab anything to eat. When I'd finally finished, armed with a camera that contained photographic evidence for my client, it was too late for any decent restaurant to be serving supper. And I just hadn't felt like eating alone.

Maybe it had been what my mother said the

previous night, or maybe just the depressing fact that I'd practically been living at the office for the past several weeks, going home only to change clothes. Perhaps it was the fact that there wasn't a warm body at home who would notice that I was never there. Not even a cat, not even a plant.

The unwelcome thought made my fingers stumble, and I hit the wrong keys. Sighing, I cranked the paper wheel back to see my mistake. I blew out a frustrated breath, then lined the paper back up and backspaced over my mistakes. I hit the X button three times in a row, then got back to typing the report again. I hated typing and had a self-imposed five mistakes per page rule. I wasn't even a quarter of the way down this page and I was down to two possible mistakes left. I concentrated as hard as I could so that I wouldn't have to redo the entire thing.

I was just cranking the wheel again to pull out the finished four-mistake page when there was a knock at the door. I peered at my desk clock and noticed that it was already twelve thirty. Jack was late.

"Come in." Jack's form was sharply silhouetted against the frosted door because of the hallway light. It was a nice feature, giving me a good idea of who was on the other side of the door before opening it. Since it was Jack and I was expecting him, I'd left the door unlocked.

The knob turned, and the door creaked open. Jack

walked through and made his way directly to my leather couch, slumping down into it as though he was thoroughly exhausted. His hat tipped forward and down when he hit the couch, so I couldn't see his face. Instead I looked away from the paper I was holding and took in his overall appearance. His charcoal-colored trench coat was a bit creased and had slush stains rimming the hem. His shoes were covered with muddy splashes and even his hat looked a bit dusty. The cuffs of his pants were just the slightest bit tatty, and overall he looked like he'd been working hard without a lot of rest.

"Tired?" I asked the question even though I already knew the answer.

"It's not enough to say I'm tired. Exhausted, delirious, or drained maybe, but nothing so trivial as tired."

Welcome to my world, I thought. As someone who had spent the last decade of my life subsisting on as little sleep as the human body could survive on, I understood that feeling precisely.

"You sure you're up to going over all this stuff tonight then?"

"Half the reason I'm so tired is that when I go to bed, I can't sleep at all for thinking of Maggie. I have to know what you've found out."

I picked up his file from the corner of my desk and opened it to my report sheet. It felt strange to treat Jack like a client, but I wanted to keep this as official as possible. "I'll start by telling you what I don't know. I don't know where she lives now, I don't know if she's married, and I haven't been able to track down a birth certificate under her name for the child."

"What were you able to find out?" His voice was tight, and I tried not to think how hard this conversation was on him.

"She is no longer with the Army; she resigned her position last year. Instead, as of last report she was working at one of the hospitals in Berlin. I'm not sure why she hasn't left, because Berlin is not a safe place to be these days. Although given her service record, I'm not sure safety is much of a priority with this woman."

"And that's it?"

I didn't even need to hear the disappointment in his voice to know that this was not the information he was hoping for. "I have no contacts in Germany. I'm only able to find out things that are already public information." I weighed my words carefully before allowing them to form. "I know it goes against the grain, but I think you should wait until she either writes you back or you have more information to work with. This just isn't enough to be of any real use."

"What if I pull some FBI strings to see if I can contact her? I can go through the back channels, keep it really quiet." I knew he was desperate, but nevertheless his words sent a shock through me.

"Great idea. And maybe you can be arrested and put on trial as a spy." I slammed my hand against the desk, appalled that he'd even mention it as a possibility. "You already know this, Jack, that's why you came to me in the first place. As an agent of the US government, you cannot have contact with someone who could possibly be, or at least appear to be, a foreign enemy agent. Not only would it kill your career, it could land you in jail for treason. Let me keep looking; maybe there's some avenue of pursuit that I haven't considered yet."

He shoved off his hat then ran his fingers through his hair. "No. I know you've done your best; I think I'm just going to have to go and find her if I ever want to be able to sleep again." I checked his eyes and saw the grim determination in them.

My heart stuttered in my chest. "You know what that means. There has to be another way, an angle we haven't looked at, something."

Jack shook his head slowly. "I know exactly what it means, but I don't think I have a choice."

"Jack, you can't walk into Berlin, get Maggie, save her from whatever trouble she's in, and just walk back into your old life again."

This time it was Jack whose control slipped. His fist pounded against the arm of the couch next to him. "I know that. I know the FBI will fire me. I've already asked for a temporary leave of absence and been denied. The next step is booking myself a ticket to Germany and handing in my letter of resignation."

I shoved myself up from my desk, heart pounding and frustrated beyond measure. "You can't do this. You can't throw away your entire career on some woman that you haven't seen in years and that you don't know really needs rescuing. It's all speculation at this point. If she really needed you, the least she could have done was write you a letter that explained something, instead of the cryptic few lines she did send."

Jack grabbed his hat off the couch next to him and jammed it back on his head. "I don't expect you to understand," he muttered, then stopped. "Actually, yes, Allie, I do. Of anyone in the world, it would be you that I would expect to understand what I'm going through. She's not just some woman, she's *the* woman. I have no choice in this. I wish you could see that."

"Believe me, I do see how hard this must be, but it's not like the FBI is just going to let you go. Even if you quit, they're not going to let a former agent of the US government into Berlin and give him the opportunity to pass along or sell secrets to the Russians. You'd be stopped before you made it into the city, and they wouldn't just send you home. They'd put you into federal custody and interrogate you before deciding if they could find enough evidence to try you."

"What do you think I'm thinking about all those hours when I can't sleep? I'm not stupid. I know how these things work, and I'm certainly smart enough to come up with a plan that could get me in and out of Berlin without being caught." Anger slipped through his voice now.

"It's not you I'm doubting Jack, it's this woman. How do you know you can trust her? What if she is out to compromise you? What if you get caught? Think of the risks you'd be taking, just to find the woman who left you the last time." The last words came out as a shout, and the second they left my mouth I wished for them back. The office went dead silent. All I could hear was the tick of the clock counting as the seconds clicked by without either of us speaking. "I'm sorry. That was uncalled for. I wasn't there. I don't know what really happened, I'm just—"

"No, you don't know, Allie. And the only thing I know is that this is something I have to do. With or without your help." He shoved himself off the couch and cleared the room in three strides. He left without another word and slammed the door behind him.

I slumped against the desk, head in my hands. Regret seeped in through every pore. I had handled that badly. I'd known that he wouldn't want to hear my assessment of the situation, but I'd had no idea that I would be so upset at the idea of Jack running in blindly to save this woman. I'd been too blunt; I'd tried to give him advice he didn't want to hear. And the ironic part was that I would do exactly the same thing Jack was contemplating doing. I would head to Berlin without a plan, regardless of the risk, if David were there.

I sat for a long time at my desk trying to put a name to the sick feeling in my stomach. It was about three in the morning when it came to me. Envy.

Chapter 7

I DIDN'T SLEEP at all that night. Didn't even close my eyes, just lay on my office couch staring at the ceiling and wondering how I could possibly be jealous of a woman I'd never met and a man I knew I'd never love. At least not in a romantic sense. But Jack was my "almost." If I could have loved anyone but David, it would have been Jack. We got along, we understood each other, we had common interests, he never seemed to look down on me because I was a woman. The man could even make me laugh. I'd taken him home for dinner with my parents, but there was still some corner of my heart that not even Jack with all of his wonderful qualities could fill. And yet, I was jealous. Not logical, but fact.

I shook my head and then rubbed my eyes. Exhausted from three days in a row with less than two hours of sleep a night, I was ready to crash onto the nearest flat surface and sleep until I wasn't tired anymore.

Unfortunately, I was nowhere near a bed. Instead I was in a subway car, heading up to Jack's office. I blew on my gloved fingers, trying to keep them from stiffening up with the cold. Every time there was a stop, and the doors slid open to let in a crowd of commuters, a fresh blast of cold air came rushing toward me. I closed my eyes and tried to imagine the stifling heat of summer, the baking feeling of the sun's rays bouncing off the concrete.

It didn't help. I blew on my fingers and tried to keep my mind on other things. Rehearsing my apology to Jack mostly. I understood exactly why he was ready to quit, to leave everything behind, in order to find her.

After last night, I doubted that he would be eager or even happy to see me, which is why I hadn't called first. I knew that he always started his mornings at the FBI field office, no matter where the investigation of the day might take him after that. I could only hope that I'd timed it right. It was a little after seven a.m., and I would probably get to his office a little before seven thirty.

I'd had most of the night to think about what to say to him, but I still wasn't sure of the best tack to take. All I knew is that I had to make things right between us.

When I arrived outside his building there was already a steady stream of trench-coated and fedoraed men heading inside. I looked around to see if

I could spot him, but all of the faces and walks were unfamiliar to me. The snow and slush soaked into my leather shoes as I stood on the sidewalk, trying to decide if I should wait for him here or go inside. Undecided for a moment, I took another look around. It was the cold that propelled me into the building when my second sweep of the area didn't find him either. I knew I wouldn't be able to get very far into the building without an official FBI escort, and if Jack was already up there I wasn't sure exactly how I could get to him.

Despite not knowing how to proceed, I was grateful to get into the building. The lobby was filled with milling people and was warm enough to make me sigh in relief. I plucked at the tips of my gloved fingers one by one until I had both gloves off, then stuffed them into my pocket. Time to face Jack.

I took the elevator to his floor, ignoring the crush of black-suited men around me. Jack had once told me that every FBI agent is given a budget when he is hired, specifically for black suits, white shirts, black ties, and black shoes. Every single man in the elevator right now was dressed in that precise uniform. As far as I could see it would make it rather hard to work undercover. I shook off the thought and brought my mind back to why I was here, surrounded by Feds. I shifted and watched the elevator numbers light up as we ascended and mentally tried to work out what I needed to say.

I wanted to tell him only that I was sorry, but

not the reasons behind it. How could I possibly explain to him the confusion of what I was feeling? How could I confess my envy of a woman I'd never met? I shoved the thoughts out of my mind, determined to do this one step at a time. The first step would be getting access to Jack in the first place. The elevator dinged for his floor, and I had to maneuver past a few others who stood between me and the elevator doors. Once I was off, I turned down the hallway Jack and I'd traveled the last time he'd brought me to this building. After about fifteen feet of hallway it bottle-necked because two guards blocked the way.

These men would not let me pass. I already knew that. Knew how much of an effort it had been for Jack to get me in before. There had been special clearances needed, badges and permission. Even then I'd only been taken to a deserted office. Without any of those special access permissions I had no chance of getting by these guards now. I came here with no invitation, and I had no idea if there was any way I could get a message to Jack. But I had to try.

Chapter 8

THE GUARDS moved together, blocking my way and my view of the hallway beyond them. The one on the right stepped forward slightly. "Ma'am?"

I tried not to look like a threat. I knew most men

didn't perceive me as one anyway, often to their detriment, but these two stared at me through hostile eyes.

"I'd like to get a message to Jack O'Connor, please."

The guard didn't even blink. "I'm sorry, that's not possible, ma'am. I suggest you try telephoning him." As soon as he was done speaking he raised his eyes and stared somewhere beyond my head.

I gritted my teeth. I was not going to go all the way back to my office just to call Jack to come out of his office to talk to me. "I don't need to go in to speak to him, I just need you to let him know that I'm here. I'm waiting for him." I raised my eyebrow. "I have information for him, and I guarantee you, he will want to speak to me." I gave the guard my best "I'm not leaving" glare. There were several long moments of frustrated silence on both sides before the guard sighed. "Your name, ma'am?"

I tried not to let the relief show on my face. "Miss Fortune. Allie Fortune." I corrected myself almost instantly, but not soon enough to stop the wince that came with saying my name out loud. Miss Fortune. I sometimes wondered if my life would have been different if I'd had a different last name instead of one that made me feel as though I were jinxed.

I drew myself out of my thoughts when I saw the guard murmur something to his silent compatriot before walking down the special access hallway. The remaining guard took a half step to the side, presumably to block me from forcing my way through, and I nearly laughed. He was probably a foot taller than me, had three times my strength, and was carrying a gun. Still, he was trained to view me as a threat. It was both a bit comical and a little satisfying. I merely stood, arms folded, waiting for Jack to appear. I could only hope I hadn't missed his daily office check-in.

We stood there, staring each other down like adversaries for about five minutes before the second guard came back. He stepped back into his place seamlessly. I raised my eyebrow at him.

"Special Agent O'Connor will be out in a few minutes to see you." Both guards then resumed their brick wall duties and didn't look at me again. Feeling invisible, but relieved, I waited.

Jack appeared five minutes later, and I knew immediately that something catastrophic had happened. His face was chalky, a mask of worry. I took a moment to pray that he hadn't done anything rash like quit his job. A replay of our argument flowed through my brain, but I immediately dismissed it as a possible cause of the desperate look on Jack's face. It was something much, much worse.

My rehearsed apology died in my throat. He didn't speak; instead he just came to me, grasped me by the elbow, and led me to the elevator.

We were both silent as the elevator slid down to the lobby. There were people in the car with us, and they spoke softly to each other, but I knew better than to say anything. The shattered look on his face was the only warning I needed. We stood side by side, but we could have been strangers sharing nothing more than an elevator car.

When the elevator doors hissed open at the main floor, Jack grasped me by the elbow again and steered me out of the building. He led me to a coffee shop directly across the street. We were seated in the vinyl booth before either of us broke the silence.

"What happened?" My apology could wait. It seemed almost trivial now.

He didn't speak. Instead he pulled an envelope out of his suit coat pocket. He handed it to me before finally breaking his silence. "This should have been first. The letters must have crossed in the mail." He then motioned for me to read it.

Chapter 9

MAGGIE, NOVEMBER 1947

HER BACK RESTED against frigid concrete. Weary and close to tears, she let her body sag for a moment as she tried to categorize the level of disaster that had befallen them both. Huddled in a stairwell, homeless, penniless, and running—it wasn't good. Maggie took a deep breath and tried to think. She felt the child at her side slip into an exhausted sleep and breathed a prayer of thankfulness. *Thank You, Father, that we are safe. Please show me how to protect the precious daughter You've given me and help me to listen for Your voice directing me. I know that You care for us both and that it is Your will that I trust You. Even with my life. Even with the life of my child.*

Maggie opened her eyes and wiped at the flowing tears with the back of her hands. Despite the fact that both their lives were in danger she felt a mist of peace descend on her and still her desperate thoughts.

Jack.

The name sprang fully formed to the front of her mind. There was no mistaking the voice. It resonated in her heart and her mind and brought goose bumps out on her skin. She shivered and rubbed her hands along her arms.

Are You sure? He probably never wants to hear my name again. I hurt him so badly before.

Ask him to come.

The words whispered across her mind, and she knew she had to try.

Chapter 10

THE ENVELOPE looked just like the one Jack had showed me several days ago. The postmark and handwriting were both the same. Dread spread through me, coating my mouth with the coppery taste of fear. I looked back at Jack, but he just waited for me to read.

I pulled out a sliver-thin folded page.

Jack,

I've tried to write this letter in my mind at least a hundred times today, but I still don't know how to start. After all the years we've been apart, why should I have the right to ask anything of you? I have no answer to that, other than to say that I've never forgotten you, or needed you more than I do right at this moment.

I'm in trouble, big trouble. And having lived and worked in some very frightening places over the past five years, I can say with all assurance that I've never been in more danger than I am right now. And if it was only me, perhaps I would have talked myself out of writing this letter, but it's not just me. There's a child.

An eight-year-old girl, an orphan, Greta. We found each other one day in this desolate city and neither of us had anyone else, and we've been together ever since. There's so little I can risk telling you right now. There's no way to keep communications private in this country so I can't go into any of the details of my situation in this letter. I just have to ask you to trust me. We're talking about life and death.

Once, many years ago, we trusted each other completely. I'm asking you to trust me like that again now. I need you. If you can come to Berlin as soon as you get this letter, you can leave a message for me at the airfield at the edge of the French-controlled sector of Berlin. I'll find you.

Always,
Maggie.

I looked up at Jack and watched as he folded the letter and set it down on the table in front of him. His expression was haunted but determined. "I'm going. I'll be on the next flight over."

I understood the sentiment, but I had to make him see reason. I waited for several seconds, trying to plan my words carefully. "I understand the desire to rush out and hop on the first plane to Berlin, but can we just think about this for a minute?"

I reached out and laid my hand across his. "I'm not saying don't go. Not at all. But I'm your friend, and you've hired me as your P.I. That gives me the right and the obligation to help you think clearly right now."

I tried a hesitant smile, but he didn't smile back. I sighed and took it as a good sign that he didn't pull his hand away from mine.

"Just let me be your friend right now. There are some things that you will have to do before you can go. First off, you have to find a way to get into Germany without making the US government think you're a traitor. Officially you have no business being there, and it's going to take a lot for you to even get into the country without being led back onto a plane in shackles. So the first thing we have to do is figure out how to get you in. The next thing we're going to have to do is get cash, passports, and everything you're going to need to get her out once you're actually there. From what I can guess from the letter, she needs to get out of Berlin, her and the child"—I paused—"which I don't think is even legal. You're not going to be able to just book her a ticket and fly out. It's going to be more complicated and probably a lot more expensive than that."

I continued, "You're going to have to quit your job. If you choose to do this—" I shook my head. "Don't glare at me. It's still a choice. You don't have to go. I'm not saying you shouldn't, but I am saying that you still have choices." I hesitated, not sure how to proceed. I knew it needed to be said, but I didn't want to be the one to say it. I took a deep breath and just forced the words out. "What if she needs your help to get back to America, but once she's here she doesn't want to be here with you?"

I closed my eyes. The question needed to be asked, but I still hated myself for asking it. To my surprise, Jack didn't seem to be stumped by this one. In fact, of all the questions I'd raised in the past five minutes I think this was the one he actually knew the answer to.

"It doesn't matter. Whether she is only contacting me because she has no one else to turn to or not, it doesn't matter. All I know is that I have to do this. And whatever happens after, happens."

I let my disbelief show on my face. "Are you sure?"

"David is alive. You know this. What if he needed your help? Would you base your decision to help or not help on why he hasn't tried to contact you?"

My stomach creased into tangled knots, but I wouldn't be swayed. "This isn't about me. It's about what this will do to you if it doesn't turn out the way you want it to."

Jack shoved off his hat and scrubbed his hand through his hair. "I have no choice. Whatever's going to happen is going to happen."

I leaned back and balled my napkin in my fist. "Fair enough, but you know I had to ask."

Jack blew out his breath and fiddled with the brim of his hat. "Yeah, I understand. And someday I'll thank you for it. Probably not today, but someday."

His words made me smile, as they were meant to, and I gave his hand a squeeze before pulling away. His eyes had some of the old spark back to them.

"I'm going to ask you a favor."

Jack's eyes went cautious. "Okay."

"Don't make any plans yet. I mean, hand in your resignation and take care of things on the work end, but don't do any more than that today. Give me the day to get some information together, and then tonight you can come by the office, and we'll try to put together a plan that's going to work."

He started to protest.

"The better plan you have going in, the more chance you'll have at success. You know this. Let me help you, Jack." I looked into his eyes, imploring him to listen to reason. He held my gaze for several long seconds before nodding once.

"I'll get things wrapped up at work, and I'll come by your office around six. Is that enough time for you?"

Less than ten hours. Not even close to enough, but I nodded anyway. "Do me a favor though.

Bring something for supper. It's probably going to be a long night, and I don't want to have to go out."

"I'll stop by the restaurant and get something from there."

I knew he was talking about his family's restaurant, and I also knew that I could count on an extra hour he would be delayed there. Stopping by to see his mother would never take less than an hour, and I needed every minute I could get.

I nodded. "Sounds good."

Jack shoved his hat back on and levered himself out of the booth. The waitress had never even made it over to take our order, so there was no bill to pay.

"I'm off to tie up loose ends at work. I'll see you tonight." With that he walked away.

"You're off to quit your job and turn your back on everything you've ever worked for, you mean." I said the words under my breath at his retreating back, but I understood what he meant when he said he didn't have a choice.

Chapter 11

BY SIX O'CLOCK I had some solid information. I'd been on the phone and making notes almost all day with one quick trip to talk to a former client, and at last had the bones of a plan for getting in and out of Berlin safely. I could only hope Jack would be willing to listen. I typed out all of the information I'd gathered and put together a to-do list in the event we decided to go with the plan I'd come up with.

In the middle of tapping out the details of my plan, the phone rang. I glanced at the clock, wondering what the chances were that Jack had thought better of our deal and was calling me from the airport right now. I closed my eyes and prayed that I was wrong.

"Allie Fortune."

"Is that any way to answer the phone, Alexandra? You sound like a dock worker."

I sighed and turned away from the typewriter. "Hello, Mother."

"I'm calling to reschedule dinner. You and Jack had to leave early the other night, so I'd like you to come by another night. To make up for the dinner we missed."

I'd been expecting something like this, but even I was surprised by how she could make it sound as though we'd had to leave early because of a previous engagement or something, not because of a family fight at the dinner table. I shook my head and mentally added another skill to my mother's impressive list of diplomatic abilities. She was a true master of rewriting history to suit her needs. It took me a second to form an appropriate response. "You mean the dinner when you were so rude that Jack and I had to leave? Is that the dinner you're talking about?"

There was a second of silence. "There's no need for sarcasm, Alexandra. It was an off night for everyone. I think we should just look past it and move forward. You're welcome to bring Mr. O'Connor with you, as well."

A whole range of responses filtered through my mind, but I bit my tongue and waited for the right one. Despite the direction of our entire relationship since I'd been old enough to talk, I didn't actually like being at odds with my mother. "Should I consider this an apology, then?"

There was silence on the other end of the line. Instead of waiting for a response, I barreled ahead. "I'm sorry too, Mother. I agree. Let's put it behind us."

"Oh. All right then." Apparently she had been ready for a fight and now she didn't seem to know what to say. "About dinner then?"

"I'm afraid that's going to be a problem. I'm actually going to have to cancel our dinner for at least a few weeks as I'm going to be out of the country." I picked up a folder from the desk and started rearranging pages, waiting for the inevitable response.

"Oh, see, that's what I get for believing that you really are willing to put things behind us. It's just like you, Alexandra, to pull something like this—"

I interrupted her. "No, Mother. Something has come up with work. I'm going to be out of the country for at least a week or two. As soon as I'm

56

back, I'll resume with the Wednesday night dinners. I can't speak for Jack, but I'll be there."

"Where are you going?"

I knew I had to be vague or I'd never get her off the telephone. "I have to help a client with a problem. I'm flying into France and then driving to Berlin."

"Berlin?" One thing I had to say for my mother was that she was pretty open-minded about women traveling alone. She'd done it herself for years, and she'd encouraged me as a young woman to see the world as well. "Well, be careful." She sounded more distracted than worried. "Berlin's not a great place to spend a lot of time, but I'm sure everything will be all right." The words came out slowly, as though she was thinking about something else. "Although if you have to go somewhere, France is a far better choice. Though it might be better to wait until springtime."

I held back a sigh. "This is a business trip, Mother. I have to go now because I'm following up a lead."

"Of course." Her voice sharpened at that and she sounded more like herself. "Though I can't imagine what kind of case would take you all the way overseas."

I rubbed at my temple with the end of my pencil. A throbbing headache had sprung up, full-blown, over the course of the phone conversation.

"I need to go now, Mother. I'm expecting a client

to arrive any minute." I rolled right over her sputtering attempts to keep the conversation going. "I'll phone you as soon as I'm back. I promise."

I set the phone back into its cradle and blew out a breath. I'd been dreading that call for days. It hadn't gone nearly as badly as I'd imagined.

I leaned back in my wooden chair, stretching my shoulders back and trying to loosen the muscles that had been pulled tight with tension all day. I was in the middle of a neck roll when there was a knock on the door.

I gave my neck and shoulders one last stretch before calling, "Come in."

The door rattled open, and Jack let himself in.

He flipped off his hat and threw it toward the hat stand. I almost clapped when it landed on a hook, circled for a second, and then settled. He grinned, and for half a moment I was fooled. But when he crossed the room to set the food on the desk, I got a good look at his face, his eyes. He looked awful. His sparkle was gone, eyes dull, smile forced so that it was probably closer to a grimace. If I was any judge I'd say that Jack was just barely holding it together.

"Did you tell your mother?" I stood up, rounded my desk, and took the box of food he still carried from his hands.

"Did I tell her what?" He removed his coat and avoided my eyes.

I set the box on my desk and turned back to him. "Did you tell your mother that you quit your job, that you've heard from Maggie, that she's in danger, or that you're going to Berlin to help her?"

He looked away and started unpacking the food, laying out the plates and cutlery. "No. I didn't tell her any of that."

"What did you tell her then?"

"I told her that I wouldn't be around for a while. That I'd be away on a job for a few weeks. She's used to that kind of thing."

"You're not planning on telling her?"

He looked up and his expression told me to drop it, but I ignored it.

"What if—" I didn't want to finish the sentence.

"What if I don't come back? What if things end badly?" He finally met my eyes, and I saw that my questions were making him angry, but I kept pushing anyway.

"It's not like you're just going out for dinner. You're headed into one of the most dangerous places in the world, without the benefit of the FBI behind you, and you're going in basically blind. That's not quite what I'd call a low-risk proposition. I think you should tell her." I crossed my arms and waited for him to respond.

Jack just shook his head and kept unpacking. "Not going to happen. Next subject."

His voice was tight like he was close to the edge, and I decided not to push it further. For the moment it seemed like we were going to try to pretend everything was okay. I sighed and tried to put myself in his place. He really looked like he could use an hour with no conflict, so I simply rounded to my side of the desk and started to fill my plate.

The lasagna smelled great, and I knew from experience that Jack's mom was a wonderful cook, but I wasn't truly hungry. The food was more like a prop between us, something to do with our hands while we took a moment.

I wondered how he was going to take the news that I was going with him to Germany.

Chapter 12

WE ATE MOSTLY in silence. Jack somehow seemed both impatient and reluctant to get down to the business of figuring out how to get into and out of Berlin. But by the time the food was gone, I had most of what I needed to say to him worked out in my mind.

"You ready?" I returned my plate to the box, pulled a file off the top of my pile, flipped through the pages, and waited for his go-ahead. Jack nodded, shoved his own dishes aside, picked a pen up off my desk, and started fiddling with it.

"Ready."

I sighed and could only hope that he'd be willing to hear me out completely. I had the feeling that he wanted to arrive in Berlin, sword drawn, banner waving, but I was going for a far more subtle approach.

"All right. I've done lots of research today, and I've come up with a way to get into Berlin and to get out with, if all goes well, Maggie and Greta." I felt a surge of hope as I said this. I could only hope Jack would see the benefits of this plan too.

He leaned back and seemed to slide into professional mode. The mode I was used to seeing Jack in. He was a great FBI agent and investigator, and it was a relief to see him like that again. For the past few days Jack had been operating mostly on fear and instinct.

"It's not necessarily going to be that hard to get into Berlin, it's getting out that's going to be the problem. Most especially, getting out with a German orphan. Fortunately there are a few very plausible reasons for Americans to move in and out of Berlin with a child in tow."

Jack's eyebrow winged up but he remained silent. I took that as a good sign and continued.

"There are war orphans all over Germany, and a law was passed about a year ago so that charitable organizations like churches could send over representatives to select and bring groups of orphans back to the US for formal adoptions."

"Which would make it easy to get a certain orphan out." Jack's face lit up with understanding. He dropped the pen and leaned back in his chair.

"Easier." I didn't want to leave the wrong

impression. "Not even close to easy. Things are chaotic in Germany, and all it would take is an officious government man refusing us entry to derail our plans. Also, papers need to be filed with the German government for the people coming over to pick up the orphans. These people have to be church-sponsored, then approved by the German government."

Jack's face fell. "All of those things take time. Time we don't have." I watched as frustration etched itself around his eyes.

"But this is where I start earning my keep as your private investigator—"

"I'm not paying you anything."

I grinned. "Lucky for you then that you're going to get more than you've paid for." I thumbed the tabs of the file I was holding, trying to find a way to condense what was written inside. "I have a friend, an ex-client actually. He happens to be the minister over at the American Overseas Missions Church. I went over to speak with him this afternoon, and he and I have worked out an arrangement." I hesitated on the last words.

"What sort of arrangement?"

"He had a team from his church ready to go, but one of them has fallen sick and can't make the trip. I've offered to take their place. You and me. We can leave tomorrow."

I held my breath, waiting for his reaction.

Dead silence.

I held myself still, not giving in to the urge to fidget or explain further. I knew Jack was not going to like the idea of me tagging along, but he didn't have any other choices in this instance. I knew he was thinking it through, trying to come up with alternate scenarios in his mind.

"I could go myself, take this person's place, but alone."

"The papers are for a husband and wife team. The German government is extremely sticky about things like this."

"Husband and wife?"

I held his gaze, not willing to be the first one to look away. I was not going to let him talk me out of this or find an alternate solution. Whether he knew it or not, he needed me. "Yes, husband and wife. If you think about it, it's the perfect cover, possibly the only cover that could get you into that country unnoticed."

Jack leaned back and shook his head. "No. I won't do it like this. It's one thing for me to go over there, knowing that I could be walking into a minefield; it's entirely another to ask you to come along with me."

"You haven't asked. I offered. And it's really your only chance, Jack. From the sound of that letter, she doesn't have months to sit around waiting for you. If you agree to this, I can get the paperwork in order, and we can leave tomorrow night." That was my trump, the unbreakable reason we had to go with my plan, speed. Do it my way and we can leave tomorrow.

"And what's in it for you? Why do you care so much?"

The question hit me like an open-handed slap. I'd been asking myself the same thing for days now, but I didn't have a coherent answer. I knew in my gut why, but it wasn't something I could sort out into words. Especially not to Jack himself.

I decided rather than trying to explain, I would throw the question back at him. "If it were me, and I had to go to find David, would you let me go alone?"

He opened his mouth as though he were going to try to deny that he would insist on coming, but he couldn't do it. He closed his mouth and glared at me. "It's not the same thing, and you know it. I don't need protection." He looked angry and frustrated, and I had the feeling he was starting to see that he was cornered. He needed to leave; I had the means and the method. He wasn't going to be able to go around me on this.

I didn't believe entirely that he didn't need protection, but I didn't say so. Instead I tried to make him understand. "I'm coming as backup. As your partner. Someone to watch your back for you."

I could see he wasn't convinced. "Jack, you're a good friend, one of my best friends. Let me do what I can. You'd do the same for me." I was fairly sure of it.

"I would. Without question, but I can't ask you to do this for me. It's not right."

"I've told you before. You're not asking. The arrangements are made; it's the best way. Let me help you, Jack."

Ten nerve-wracking seconds of silence passed before Jack spoke. "Tell me your plan. All the details. Then we'll see."

I outlined the whole thing to Jack, and by the time I was done, I was sure I'd convinced him. His face betrayed no reaction, but my plan was really the best we could do on such short notice. If everything worked out the way we hoped, we stood an excellent chance of succeeding.

Jack leaned back in his chair, uncrossed his arms, and sighed. It was a sigh of defeat, and I felt a big grin cross my face.

"You're right. It's a good plan. And it's not like I have any other choices. It would take months to come up with anything better."

"So we're partners again?"

Jack winced. "Looks like it. Although, run that married part by me again."

I felt a flush crawl up my cheeks. "We're going in place of a married couple. I can change the names on the documents, but they were filled out for a man and woman. A married man and woman."

"We're going to Berlin as husband and wife?"

"Looks like it, Mr. Fortune." It was either laugh

65

or crawl underneath the desk in embarrassment, so I tried to laugh.

"Why not Mr. and Mrs. O'Connor?" Jack's face was impassive, giving me no idea how he was taking all of this.

"O'Connor is a fairly common name, but even then it's not wise to use it when we're trying to cross into a country where you have no business being. So, it makes sense that we become Mr. and Mrs. Fortune."

"What about my identification, passport and such?"

"It'll be ready by tomorrow. And don't ask me any more about it. Just believe me when I say that you'd be happier not knowing."

Jack winced and ran a hand over his face. "You know where to get a fake passport on twenty-four hours notice?"

"I hang around with classy people. What can I say?"

Jack and I went our separate ways about an hour later. Jack had me go over the plans once more, and we made a few minor changes. We both had a mountain of things to do in order to be ready to leave the next night. Jack was financing the trip, so he had to get cash from the bank. US currency would help us in Berlin as reichsmarks were almost worthless. We also needed black-market items to use for trade. Four cases of Hershey chocolate bars would be my bargaining chips of preference. Cigarettes were another sought-after item on the German black market, but I'd much rather have chocolate to distribute at the orphanages than cigarettes. So I had to see a man about a passport, buy cases of chocolate, pack, and take out some cash of my own, just in case.

At my desk, I shuffled file folders and made phone call after phone call, informing my clients that I had to make an emergency trip but would be back in two weeks. I still had a few stray papers lying around, and I picked them up, preparing to file them in the appropriate folders, when a manila envelope caught my attention.

I sank back into my chair. I pulled the paper from its tight confines, and my breath backed up as though I'd never seen it before. But I had. I'd read the photostatted page at least a thousand times, despite the fact that there was so little readable information on the sheet. Line after line had been censored, thick black ribbons crossing out information I was desperate to have, but the most important information hadn't been obscured. The affirmation that my instincts had been right and that David was still alive. But that was the only thing the document told me. I shoved the paper back into the envelope and put it into the bag I was packing.

I finished my phone calls to clients and then made the most important call, to the airline. Reserving two tickets to Paris took far more time than it should have, but when I hung up I knew that Jack and I were well and truly committed now. I felt no regret, just a faint sense of trepidation.

I worked feverishly getting arrangements made and sighed in frustration when there was a knock at my door. If it was anyone other than Jack, I was going to have to tell them to go away.

"Come in," I called.

The door swung open, and I looked up to see my mother standing in the doorway. My jaw fell open for an instant, but immediately I forced myself to don a neutral expression.

"Well, this is a first," I said, trying to sound casual. She looked like she was dressed for tea with royalty, and the slight wrinkling of her nose let me know that my office did not measure up to her standards. To tell the truth, her judgment didn't bother me. I rather enjoyed watching her mentally debate if it would go against the rules of etiquette to remain standing the entire time she was here. I didn't blame her. I wouldn't want to get dust or something worse on that very expensive suit either.

She looked around the room, cataloguing each piece of furniture and every out-of-place file, I was sure. After a few seconds she turned to me. "Yes, it is a first. I had a dreadful time finding this place. The taxi driver told me that this was the right place, but I was sure no daughter of mine would have an office in this neighborhood, never mind this building."

She looked around the room again. "It would appear that I was wrong."

I sighed. I wasn't up for this today. "Is there a reason you picked today to make your first trek to my office, Mother?"

She looked around one last time before sitting gingerly on the chair in front of my desk. I fought the urge to tidy my desk or shift the stack of papers I had in front of me. It didn't seem to matter how old I got, my mother still had the power to intimidate me. Instead I shored up all of my professionalism and placed my hands on the desk, one on top of the other, and waited for her to tell me why she'd come.

My stillness seemed to make her uncomfortable. She shifted in her chair and took a deep breath before speaking. "Alexandra, when I heard you were going to Berlin I realized that this would be the perfect opportunity for me to do something I've been wanting to do for several years."

For one horrible second I thought she was going to tell me that she wanted to come with me.

"I need to hire you, or whatever it is that people do when they want to engage your investigative services."

If she had reached across the desk and slapped me I would have been no less surprised.

"You can't hire me." I shook my head. Funny, those words had been coming from me a lot lately.

She leaned forward, her eyes narrowed, voice

69

cold. "I can certainly afford your fee, Alexandra, if that's what you're implying."

I shook my head in frustration. "No, that's not what I said. Or what I meant. You don't have to hire me, and you know it. If you need me to do you a favor or look into a matter for you, all you have to do is ask."

She shook her head. "No. That's entirely unacceptable. Let me be blunt, Alexandra. I would like to keep this particular task on a purely professional level. You are going to Berlin, you are a professional private investigator, as you are so happy to continually remind me, and I happen to have the need of a professional private investigator who is going to Berlin."

I leaned back in my chair and tried to figure out what was going on in her head. "I will happily do what you ask, but I'm not taking your money, Mother."

She scowled at me. "Something then. I am not going to be in your debt over this."

I considered for a long moment. I'd never even dared dream of being in this situation. My mother willing to bargain with me. It took only seconds for me to know exactly what I wanted from her. "All right, no more blind dates. Ever. That's my price." I had to fight to keep the look of triumph off my face. This was so much better than any monetary fee ever could be.

She stared at me, her eyes narrowed, before

finally nodding. "Fine. Have it your way. I accept your terms."

I couldn't keep the grin of satisfaction from spreading across my face. "All right then. Why don't you tell me what you need me to look into?"

My mother, for her part, kept the meeting strictly formal, exactly how she would deal with any other service person she'd hired to perform a task for her. I had no problem with that and was actually quite eager to hear what she needed my services for.

She placed a bag on the desk and pulled out a beautiful wooden box. I picked it up. It was featherlight and varnished to a lustrous glow. The top of the box had a painting, no, a mosaic made of different colors of inlaid wood in the pattern of a Japanese woman in traditional dress. It was a beautiful piece, and I'd seen it displayed in our parlor for years. I'd barely ever taken a second glance at it before, but now I ran my fingers along the satin smooth wood and soaked in the piece's beauty.

"I need you to take this box and give it to a man I once knew in Berlin. He was a priest at St. Martin's cathedral before the war. I have no idea if he has retired, if he's still the priest there, or if he is even still alive. He was an old man when I knew him, so it's very possible that he could be no longer with us."

I sat up in my seat. "You want me to deliver this

box to some priest you haven't seen in years? Why?"

"I didn't realize it was necessary to reveal to a private investigator why a person wanted a job done, just that a person needed it done."

I blew out a breath. She loved to make things difficult. "I don't need to know exactly why you need this job done, but it would be helpful if I knew the circumstances. Like is the priest going to know why I'm giving this to him, is there anything about the box that could cause me trouble at the border, things like that."

My mother waved her hand airily. "None of those things will be a problem. If the priest is still alive, he will remember me and the box, and as for crossing borders, it's just an objet d'art. It's not stolen or bought off the black market, if that's what you're implying."

I fought the urge to roll my eyes. That had not been what I'd been thinking or implying, and she knew it. But apparently she was in the mood to make this as difficult as possible.

I pulled the box toward me. "Fine, if you can give me the last known address of the priest, his full name, and any other information that you think might help me find him, I will do my best to deliver this—" I looked at it—"objet d'art to him."

Chapter 13

TECHNICALLY JACK wouldn't be at risk of imprisonment for treason until we crossed into Germany, but that didn't stop the heavy nauseous feeling that came over me as we boarded our flight to Paris. This was the first step. In fact once Jack used his new passport, we would have both crossed the line and there was no going back.

I'd made all of the travel arrangements and knew that we'd be pressing hard over the next two days. Not only were we going to fly halfway across the world, we were only going to have a few hours to sleep before we'd start our drive through France and into Germany.

Once we got into the city, and I refused to think about what would happen if we didn't get in, we would head straight for the airfield in the French sector to find Maggie. It was a tenuous plan, relying on the promise that she'd be there, but we just had to pray that she'd be waiting for us to arrive. As I'd packed and organized I'd been surprised at my intense desire to pray for Maggie's safety, and our own.

I buckled my safety belt and watched Jack strap himself in next to me. I set the bag holding my mother's mysterious box beside me. The click of metal snapping into metal felt like a commentary on the finality of taking this step. I leaned back against the headrest and closed my eyes. The engines roared as the plane began its slow roll out onto the runway. This was only the second time I'd ever been on a plane, and it was the first time I'd ever been on a transatlantic flight, but I forced the butterflies in my stomach to behave. Of all of the things that would come in the next few days I had the feeling that a tin can hurtling itself into the air, held up over vast stretches of ocean by nothing more than lift and thrust, should be the least of my concerns.

Once the plane was in the air I slipped off to the bathroom with my purse. One of the errands I'd run yesterday had been to fill the prescription for sedatives that the doctor had given me. I'd told him I didn't want to solve my insomnia that way, but he'd pushed the prescription into my hands as I was leaving, just in case. This was that case. I couldn't even imagine what the time change between Paris and New York was going to do to my already messed-up sleep pattern, but I knew that I needed to be sharp and coherent.

I slipped a pillbox out of my purse, removed two tablets, and forced myself to swallow them. They burned all the way down, and I dreaded their effects, but it needed to be done.

I made my way back to my seat, asking the stewardess for a blanket and a pillow as I passed. I had to wedge myself between Jack's long legs and the seat to get to mine, and I collapsed into it with a sigh of relief.

"You okay?" He turned to me, a look of concern on his face.

"Fine," I replied shortly. I saw him look away, face front again, and I sighed. I knew he was just concerned about me and distressed at the whole idea of me coming with him in general. I hated the idea of relying on drugs to sleep, relying on anything really. It made me testy, but Jack didn't deserve to get the brunt of that.

"Sorry, Jack. I'm just tired. I'm going to try to sleep now, and with any luck I won't wake up until we're landing in Paris."

Jack's eyebrow winged up at my statement. He knew that I rarely got more than three hours of sleep in a row, so I knew he was questioning how I thought I'd be able to sleep all the way to France, but I laid my head back and closed my eyes to forestall any questions.

Within minutes the stewardess had dropped off a pillow and blanket. The sleeping pills were already taking effect, making me feel slow and lethargic. I was fairly sure that if I spoke, my words would come out slurred, so I turned my face away from Jack and waited for unconsciousness to claim me.

When I woke, we were still in the air. I opened eyes that felt like they'd been sandpapered and then glued shut. My mouth was dry and my brain was stuck in neutral. I checked my watch and was slightly disappointed to see that we wouldn't be landing at Le Bourget airport for at least another three hours. Still, I had definitely slept. I felt exactly like I had the one other time I'd taken sleeping pills, and I renewed my vow not to take them again except in the case of emergency. They left me feeling awful, and under normal circumstances, the trade-off just wasn't worth it.

I turned my blurry eyes to look at Jack. He was asleep, his head leaned against the headrest and face turned away from me. The interior plane lights were dimmed, and most people around us seemed to be asleep as well.

I looked out my window. Nothing but darkness. I wondered if we were over a vast lonely stretch of ocean or if we were just too high to see the lights of civilization.

"Would you like a coffee?" The quiet question from the stewardess was welcome.

I nodded.

I spent the rest of the flight staring out the window, trying to shake the feeling of depression that wanted to blanket me.

Jack came awake as we were making our descent in France. He stretched and scrubbed his face with his hands. "We're almost here. I guess this is it then."

Chapter 14

BEFORE WE'D LEFT America, before she'd even come to hire me, I'd called my mother, in the uncomfortable position of having to ask her for a favor. She'd been gracious about it, but I knew her well enough to be sure there was some sort of string attached. I couldn't see it now, but I knew it was there. Still, she'd been able to procure what we needed. A vehicle. My mother had all sorts of friends in Paris, and she'd called one of them asking if I could borrow a vehicle for a few weeks. Jack and I found it exactly where it was supposed to be in the car lot, with the key under the front mat and with a map on the driver's seat.

Jack raised his eyebrow, surprised I think at the level of organization I'd achieved on such short notice.

I answered the question he didn't ask. "I'm going to owe my mother big for this."

"She certainly can deliver." Jack opened the trunk and shoved his bags in.

I walked around to the passenger side, shoved my luggage into the backseat, stacking our boxes of chocolate along the floor and carefully laying my mother's wooden box next to them.

I got into my seat and pulled the map to me. I was going to act as navigator. I had a vague idea of how to get from France to Germany but was rather fuzzy on the actual details.

Jack shoved the key into the ignition, fiddled around for a few moments, and after a few tries, the car's engine cranked to roaring life. I unfolded the map and tried to figure out how one got from Paris to Berlin.

Jack eased the car out of the parking space and made his way out of the parking lot. When he reached the exit he turned to me. "So?" he asked.

I double-checked the map then pointed. "That way."

He nodded and pulled out. "We're off then."

It didn't take us long to leave the lights of Paris behind. From what I could tell it would take about fifteen hours of driving time to get to the outskirts of Berlin. Of course there were border crossings along the way that could slow down our travel plans by hours. Jack's new passport had passed muster so far, but we both knew that it was the border guards on the ground who were going to give us the most trouble.

Along with passports, once we arrived in Germany we were going to need travel documents. Very few civilians could get into or out of the city for any reason. Other than being a part of a military convoy, our adoption papers were definitely the best chance we had of passing through.

As he wove through the French countryside my

mind drifted to our reason for being here. I figured I'd been very patient and maybe now it was time for Jack to share a little bit about the object of our quest.

"You haven't told me very much about Maggie or your relationship. How about we use a little of this drive to fill me in?" I asked.

Jack turned to glance at me. His expression was not particularly open, but I figured with all we were both risking on this rescue effort, he owed me. "What do you want to know?"

"Start wherever you want; it's a long drive."

Jack's knuckles tightened on the wheel, but I said nothing.

"You already know that I've known Maggie my whole life. She lived in my neighborhood and was a year younger than me. Her parents died in an auto accident when she was fifteen, and she moved in with my aunt and uncle. I really noticed her for the first time shortly after that." Jack's lips twitched at the memory. "I was crazy about her, and I made a real pest of myself at my aunt and uncle's house. Must have driven them to the brink of insanity. I doubt they'd seen me as much in my entire life as they did during the years that Maggie lived there. Once I was done with high school I started pursuing the idea of working in some sort of law enforcement. When the FBI found me, I jumped at the opportunity and left for over a year, for my training. I hoped that Maggie would wait for me."

79

My eyebrows raised. A year was a long time.

"At the time it felt like I had the world by the tail. I was in love with the girl of my dreams, and I was going to be part of the most elite law enforcement agency in the country." He paused. "My year away was a fantastic experience on a professional level, but half of me couldn't wait for it to be over so that I could get back to her. Maggie graduated from nursing school in that time, and I came home as often as I could, but we were both busy with school and work. I hoped that when all was said and done and the time was right we'd get married." Jack stopped. "Obviously that's not what happened."

I cleared my throat. "Obviously." I stayed quiet after that, hoping he'd pick up the story where he'd left off, but he didn't. He just concentrated on the road, looking tense and unhappy.

It was only a few hours before we had to pass through our first border check. We were leaving France and moving into Belgium. This wasn't a border crossing I was particularly worried about, but it was still a relief once we passed through.

Jack's tension had ratcheted up to the point that it seemed to vibrate off of him. I knew it wasn't the border crossing itself that did it. "It seems to be hard for you, adjusting to being called Mr. Fortune." I tried to make a joke out of it.

Jack looked at me, but he wasn't smiling. "It has nothing to do with the name; it's the fact that I'm using a false passport and I'm doing something illegal. I could be arrested at any point now."

I hesitated for a moment, not sure he wanted to hear what I had to say. "Saving Maggie has a price, Jack. This is it."

He turned to glare at me. "I am an officer of the law, and I'm breaking the laws I swore to uphold."

I kept my eyes on him, not flinching. "Yes, you are. Are you going to be able to live with that when this is all over?"

He took one hand from the wheel and scrubbed his face. "I certainly hope so." I could still see his principles warring with his loyalty and love, but also a deep sadness in his eyes. I knew that no matter how this rescue effort ended, there would be some reconciling for Jack to do later.

We stopped for a meal at an inn somewhere in the middle of Belgium. In a few hours we'd be crossing into Germany and the border was looming like a line of decision. Once we crossed we were committed. When we finished our dinner we pulled back onto the main road.

"Okay, we've talked about me. It's your turn." It sounded like Jack was out for payback.

I laughed. "What do you want to know?"

He paused, and it made me a little nervous. "The list is way too long." He muttered. "What are you doing about your search for David? What's your plan?"

I sighed. "I'm not sure I have one anymore," I admitted. "I've found out he's still alive, but I don't have enough information to find out where he is, or why. I'm not sure I'm really any further along than I was before. I've confirmed what I already knew. He didn't die in the war. That's it. Unless I can find a way to wrangle a favor from the OSS, or whatever they're calling themselves now, I think I'm stuck." The OSS had actually disbanded a year after the end of the war, but a few years after that a new intelligence department had been birthed, now called the CIA, but it was basically the same organization. Whatever they called themselves, they had the information I needed.

Jack didn't seem to know what to say to that. I didn't know what to do about it either.

We spent the next hours of the drive in silence, the tension in the car rising higher the closer we got to the German border.

Chapter 15

WE STOPPED IN the last town before the border to fill jerry cans with fuel and stored them in the trunk. With severe shortages of all kinds in Berlin, having a supply of fuel could possibly be the difference between making a successful exit from the city and not.

Jack got behind the wheel again. There was no conversation as we approached the German border. I did my best to keep from tensing up, but the unease vibrating off of Jack was so strong it almost had its own frequency.

As we pulled up to the blockade in the road, two men in uniform carrying guns headed toward our car. I tried to swallow my fear, and I quickly wiped my hands on the grey wool of my skirt. I could hear the acceleration of my heart in my ears, and I hoped that I would be able to look calm and collected for the next few moments. I snuck a look at Jack. His face was impassive and hard. I wanted to elbow him and tell him to relax a little, as he was broadcasting what I would call his cop-face. We were just supposed to be a married couple from a Christian mission organization.

Jack rolled down his window as one of the British soldiers approached. From the passenger seat I could only see the soldier at gun level, and it was not a pleasant sight, so I focused on getting all of our identification in order. I pulled the travel documents out of the glove compartment along with the two passports. Mr. and Mrs. Fortune. The queasy feeling that came over me as I handed them to Jack brought a wash of cold terror. If for some reason Jack's passport didn't pass muster here, we would be detained and probably arrested.

Trying to hear Jack's voice over the roaring in my ears, I leaned closer and handed the little stack of identification to him. He was deep in conversation with the soldier and didn't turn to look at me.

"We're here as representatives of the American Overseas Mission Organization. We've got the proper travel documents, and we're going straight to Berlin. We should be on our way out again within a few days," he said, answering the guard's questions but not elaborating.

I saw the soldier's eyes narrow as he examined our papers, and I decided it was time to intervene.

I leaned over Jack, aiming a bright smile at the guard. He looked up at the movement, and I caught his eye. "This is so exciting, but scary too. Going into Berlin. A big adventure. Have you been there? Is it as bad as they say?" I didn't bat my eyelashes, not able to degrade myself to that extent, but the "harmless little woman" routine seemed to work. He wasn't looking at Jack and trying to figure out his instinctive law enforcement demeanor anymore. I was going to have to remind Jack he needed to tone down on the cop body language and interrogation-type answers. Our papers said he was a teacher, and he needed to do a bit better job fitting that cover.

The soldier took a step back, closed the passport he'd been examining, and handed the paperwork back to Jack. "I've been there, ma'am, and it's not what I'd call an adventure. Be careful."

I nodded fiercely, as though chastened by his words. "Thank you so much, Officer." I saw from his uniform that he wasn't an officer, but his shoulders straightened at the comment. He took a big step back from the car and caught the eye of the other soldier before waving us forward.

I didn't take a deep breath until we were completely out of sight of the border crossing. As soon as it disappeared behind a curve in the road the adrenaline seeped out of me, leaving me cold and exhausted.

I punched Jack lightly on the shoulder. "You're a lousy actor, did you know that?"

He turned to look at me. "Oh, thank you, Officer," he said in a ridiculous falsetto.

My cheeks burned, but I kept my chin up. "It worked, didn't it?"

Jack just shook his head. "Allie Fortune playing the helpless female—I never would have believed it."

My eyes narrowed. "Well, don't get used to it, 'cause you're never going to see it again."

It was another few hours of driving before we crossed into Soviet territory and drew near to Berlin. My mind wanted to wander down all of the paths of what-if, but I tried not to let my thoughts go there.

Maggie's letter instructed us to go to the airfield at the edge of the French sector of Berlin. Her instructions had been rather ambiguous, but, like everything else on this trip, we were just going to have to trust her.

Jack's map of Berlin proved to be useless. There

were clearly marked routes that should have taken us into the French district, where we needed to go, but that must have been before the war and the bombing of the city. I looked out the car window and realized that the photographs I'd seen, the accounts I'd heard, hadn't even come close to preparing me for the total destruction that surrounded us. Buildings with holes ripped into the sides. An apartment building missing an entire wall, leaving the stacked levels of apartments open to view like some strange three-sided doll house.

The streets were full of rubble. Bits of brick, rocks, twisted hunks of metal. In places there was a trail only just wide enough for a car to fit through; in other places the street appeared undamaged. Everything, even the bits of snow coating the roads and buildings, was layered with grey dust.

"Any idea where we're going?" I turned to Jack, feeling more than a little uncomfortable now. We'd come in through the west side of Berlin, into British territory, and we needed to make our way north to the French sector. Everything from here on out was pretty much unknown. I'd gotten us into this country, into this city, but I had no idea what we were going to do from here.

"I know what streets should lead us to the airfield." He looked around us. "But somehow I doubt it's going to be that easy. I have a feeling that it might take awhile to find a clear route. I think it would be smart to stop and ask for directions."

I nodded, agreeing with him. Then it hit me. I couldn't believe I'd never thought about it until then, but how were we going to communicate with anyone here? I spoke French, not German.

Jack already had his window rolled down, letting in a blast of frigid air. He scanned the area for anyone who could help. The closest passerby was a few feet away.

"Hallo. Können Sie mir helfen?" The words flew out of Jack so smoothly that my mouth dropped open. I guess he had that problem covered.

An old woman turned toward us, her eyes wary, her coat buttoned up to her throat against the cold. *"Ja?"* She took a hesitant step toward us.

"Wir müssen zum französischen Sektor kommen. Geht diese Straße durch?"

The old woman nodded. *"Das wird dicht, aber das ist passierbar."* She took another few steps closer, and I noticed that she wasn't as old as I'd first thought. She just looked exhausted and very thin.

Jack nodded. *"Vielen Dank für Ihre Hilfe."*

The woman nodded back and let the corner of her mouth curl up.

"She says that this road is passable and will get us into the French sector. Allie, would you grab two chocolate bars, please?" he said to me without turning.

I reached into the box, pulled out two bars, recognizable from their silver and brown wrappers. I saw the woman's eyes widen as I passed the bars to Jack, and he handed them out the window to her. I felt a rush of pleasure at the unrestrained joy in her eyes. For just a second her face lit up, and it eased the evidence of too many difficult days from her face.

Jack pulled his hand back in through the window. *"Danke,"* he said to the woman, then he shoved the car back into gear and picked his way slowly through the debris-strewn road.

I let him drive in silence for a few minutes. "I didn't know you spoke German."

He didn't look away from the street. "Fluently. That's one of the things the FBI did during the war. We picked up suspected German spies and interrogated them. I was one of the translators."

"Were there many spies?" I couldn't help but wonder what was truth and what was propaganda when it came to reports of German spies on American soil.

"New York was full of more intrigue and espionage during the war than you would have believed." That was all he said. I assumed that while generalities were fine, he couldn't divulge any specifics, even though it had taken place years ago.

We drove in silence after that, but I didn't mind. I kept my eyes on our surroundings. It was evening. I wasn't quite sure exactly when, given the time zones we'd crossed in the past two days. But it was probably close to the supper hour for most people. Darkness was only an hour or so away. The people who were out and about were all walking with their eyes on the ground, coats pulled tightly around them. I hadn't been outside, but from just the few minutes Jack had had the window rolled down I knew it was bitterly cold out.

I wanted to ask Jack where we were going to stay tonight, I wanted to ask how he thought Maggie was going to find us, but instead I kept quiet and watched as we made our way down through the city. When I saw the hand-painted wooden sign that said, "You are entering the French sector" with the French version painted underneath, I breathed a sigh of relief. "So where are we going?"

Jack flicked on the car's headlights to cut through the gathering dusk, then said, "She told us to go to the airfield. I'm hoping that it will become apparent why once we get there."

Clearly he had no more of a plan than I did. I could only hope that finding Maggie would be simple. I had my doubts.

Chapter 16

WHEN WE PULLED up to the French airfield I couldn't imagine how this was going to work. It was simply a landing strip, a hangar, and a few brick buildings. It was on the very edge of the city, lined on one side with thick forest, but open on the other three sides. The landing strip itself was pocked and cracked asphalt, and I doubted that it was used much. Only in emergencies, I would imagine. The entire place appeared deserted, which wasn't a surprise as night was descending quickly.

"I think we're going to have to wait until tomorrow," I said, stating the obvious.

"Let's at least take a quick walk around, see if there's any sign of her." The words were mumbled and Jack was opening the door before I even had a chance to respond.

I guessed we were going to have a little look around then.

The light had faded, but darkness had yet to completely fall. I had a flashlight in the car, but I didn't think it was a good idea to draw any unnecessary attention to ourselves. Skulking around a deserted airfield at twilight was not a great way to remain unnoticed.

I followed Jack with a sigh. We walked around the smaller buildings. I had no idea what he was looking for, but he seemed to be doing a visual sweep of the area, so I just followed along.

He saved the biggest building, I assumed it was a hangar, for last. I rubbed my arms with my gloved hands, trying to keep warm as we walked.

Jack slowed as we came to the edge of the building, and I thought for a second that we were going to head back to the car, but something stopped him in his tracks.

He touched a brick with his finger. "This is it. Her sign."

I stepped closer so I could see what he was pointing to. It was a vertical chalk marking on the brick. I moved back and saw that there were several of them, all in a row.

Surprised that he'd actually found the sign he was looking for, I took another step back.

Jack picked up a rock from the ground and put a cross hatch through the last marked brick, then let the rock drop to the ground. "There's nothing more we can do here tonight. We'll have to wait until morning."

I nodded and followed him back to the car. Again I felt the slick sensation of unease slide through my belly. Time would tell if we'd made the right decision in coming here.

"Let's just find somewhere to sleep tonight, and we can let tomorrow take care of itself," I said.

Chapter 17

MAGGIE

MAGGIE MOVED across the frozen grass, the brittle sound loud in the early morning. How many days had she done exactly this? All in the faint hope that Jack would magically appear. That two vague letters from the girl who'd loved him, then left him five years ago, would be enough to bring him to Berlin to save her.

Still, she'd looked. Every day. She walked the two miles from home to the airfield to see if he'd come, battling a mixture of hope and despair.

When she got to the eastern wall of the hangar building, she leaned down to pick up a rock. Counting bricks, she looked for the spot to make her mark. Twelve bricks up from the bottom, the month of December. Her gaze scanned along that row until she found her old marks. Fourteen of them. Starting at the seventh brick from the end, there was a faint white line on each brick, all the way to the twenty-first one. Today was the twenty-second of December, and as she prepared to etch yet another line, evidence that she'd been here, she saw something that made her heart stop. Another line, intersecting the one on the twenty-first brick.

The rock fell out of her hand and clattered to the ground.

Someone had been here. Had understood those marks. Maggie whirled around, terror pumping through her veins. Had someone discovered her rendezvous point? Were they watching her even now, setting a trap for her? Or was it just possible that he'd come? Was it even vaguely possible that he'd come halfway across the world to help her? She reached up with a shaky finger and traced the line. Was he really here?

Maggie held her palm over her heart to try to ease the wild thumping. She hadn't believed, not really, that he would come. She'd prayed, certainly, and she'd told Greta he would come, as though it were fact, but deep in her heart, she hadn't truly believed it.

She picked up the rock again and made a line on the twenty-second brick, then did something she'd never done before. She circled it. I will find you, it said.

Wait for me, I will find you.

It took hours. She waited and watched from the woods just beyond the field. But finally when it was well into the morning and her fingers and toes felt frozen clean through from the enforced inactivity, she saw a car pull up.

Heart thumping, she forced herself to stay in her hiding spot, forced herself not to go running across the open expanse between the cover of trees and the brick building. A man in a dark trench coat and hat got out of the car. He was too far away to make out more than his outline as she watched him cross to the wall. He looked up, following the markings to the very last one. Maggie watched him trace the outline of the circle on the brick, then let his hand fall to his side.

She pushed herself to her feet, ready to reveal herself, convinced it was Jack, but she stopped when he turned back to the car and motioned with his hand. Instantly the passenger door of the car swung open.

Maggie's breath heaved out. A woman, also in a dark coat and hat, stepped out of the passenger side. Even from this distance Maggie could see that she was sharp. Smartly put together, no-nonsense stride, she crossed the distance to Jack, said something quickly, then placed her hand on his back. A gesture of support that needed no interpreting.

Maggie forced her breath in and out. She thought she'd been prepared for this. That Jack could be and probably was married. It had been five years, Maggie reminded herself harshly. She'd expected no less. Hoped maybe, but she hadn't expected anything different.

She closed her eyes. *God, thank You for bringing him here. Thank You for providing for Greta and me, despite my lack of faith. Please help me to remember that I only want Jack to be happy. Help me to concentrate on the miracle You have provided, and not to dwell on the fact that it isn't quite how I envisioned it happening.*

She took a deep steadying breath.

Please help me to trust in Your perfect will.

She opened her eyes and crossed the field.

Chapter 18

ALLIE

JACK AND I ARRIVED at the wall a little after ten a.m., hoping it was enough time for Maggie to come back and see his marking on the wall. Enough time for her to realize we were here. Part of me dreaded meeting her. I'd seen a picture of her once in Jack's apartment, so I was fairly sure I'd recognize her if I saw her, but I didn't really want to meet her.

The sound of frost being crunched underfoot made me turn.

And there she stood. Tall, but soft looking, red-gold hair pulled back with wisps that managed to escape and curl around her face. Soft grey eyes looked from me to Jack, who hadn't turned yet, and showed no reaction. They held steady on me for a second before shifting back to Jack again.

"Hello, Jack." Voice low and smooth. Again, even though I was watching carefully for an emotion, some sort of reaction, I could detect none.

Jack turned and for a second, less than that, I saw relief and emotion so strong the wake of it left me stunned, but in less time than it took to blink, his eyes iced over and blocked all of his thoughts.

"Maggie." I don't think anyone else in the world would have noticed, could have heard how tightly he controlled his voice, but I heard it, and my heart tightened in sympathy for him. I hadn't imagined quite how hard this meeting might be for him.

Maggie looked at me, her eyes still guarded and remote. "Hello, Mrs. O'Connor." The words surprised me even though I had suspected that's what Maggie would guess.

I waited for Jack to correct her. "This is Allie" was all he said. I turned to look at him, but he wouldn't meet my eyes.

I looked back at Maggie and thought for a second I saw a flash of emotion in her eyes, but it was gone before I could be sure. The tension bouncing off of these two was painful. It was Maggie who finally broke the silence.

"I don't have words to tell you how grateful I am that you've come to help us. I didn't write to you lightly, and I don't think I have the right to ask you for help, Jack, but I had nowhere else to turn. So, thank you." She nodded to both of us. "I am not exaggerating when I say that you're saving both of our lives. Mine and Greta's."

Jack nodded but didn't say anything. He would have to correct Maggie's assumption about us, but I had the feeling that he was barely keeping it together right now, so explanations would have to come later. And that conversation would have to be between Maggie and Jack.

I stepped in. "We're here to help. I guess the first thing we need to do is to hear what's been going on and why you think your lives are in danger."

Maggie looked around. The area was deserted, but she lowered her voice anyway. "We can't talk in the open. First let me take you to where Greta and I are staying. We can talk there. It's safe."

For the first time I saw an emotion in her, and it came at the mention of Greta's name. It was a combination of worry and love.

"We have a car. We can take that," Jack said.

"We can't get to where we're going by car. You'll have to leave it behind."

I bit my lip. In a city where people were so poor that two chocolate bars could almost bring someone to tears I had to worry about the likelihood of our car being stolen while we were away. It wasn't my car to risk. I also knew I couldn't leave my mother's box in there. Just in case.

She seemed to understand my worry about the car. "I can help you hide it, but we need to be quick. I have to get back."

I nodded.

She took us to a grove of trees that came up to the back of one of the buildings on the airstrip. We pulled the car as far as we could into the trees. It did the job. Not hiding the car exactly, but making it less noticeable for sure. Jack locked the car up, slipping a few things into his pockets, then motioned for Maggie to lead the way.

We followed Maggie for probably two miles. We twisted and turned through a part of the city that was even more ruined than what we'd seen so far. Here there were probably ten ruined buildings for every one that looked habitable. Rubble was everywhere, and Maggie warned us to stay away from it as there might be unexploded ordnance in it. She also kept us as far away from the ruined buildings as she could. Sometimes the buildings collapsed, killing whoever was near, she explained. She was so offhand with these comments, almost as if we were tourists and she was pointing out landmarks. She reminded me of taxi drivers in New York City pointing out the Empire State building. It occurred to me that she'd been here for years, and the destruction and its aftermath were just part of the scenery for her.

If these dangers were just everyday realities to her, I had to wonder what she thought was enough of a threat that she had to get out. Whatever it was, it wasn't going to be a small problem.

Chapter 19

MAGGIE'S HOME shocked me. It was an apartment building very much like the ones she'd warned us to stay away from for fear of being caught under a collapse. She ignored the front doors, which were blocked by a heap of rubble, and walked around to the back, checked carefully to see that no one was around, and then pulled some pieces of wood out of a pile on the ground to uncover a small cement stairwell leading down into the ground. I guessed that it was the exit from a basement apartment, but if I hadn't seen her uncover it, I never would have known it was there. She motioned for us to go down first, and when we were both at the bottom stairwell she followed us, stopping to drag the wood camouflage back over the entrance from the inside.

We both stepped aside as she moved to the door. I had no idea how she was going to let us in as there was no door handle, just a hole where it should have been. I watched her pull something out of her pocket and laughed aloud when I saw that she had the missing doorknob in her hand. Both Jack and Maggie turned to look at me. Maggie held her finger to her lips and then went back to the door. She turned the knob, jiggled it a little until it caught, then pulled it toward us. I was glad we were moving inside as it was still bitterly cold out. We all shuffled in, and I held the door as it closed, letting go when it clicked softly.

Once we were inside Maggie led us farther into the dark room. We followed, inches behind her, trusting her leading in the pitch-dark room. She slid her hands along something, feeling for something none of us could see. Eventually she seemed to find it. After a few moments of her fiddling I saw the flare of a match, and she lit the wick inside a glass hurricane lamp. The room became visible in its dim glow.

I looked around. I saw a mattress in one corner, a small table in the center of the room, and two wooden spindle chairs. That was all of the furniture. Along the back wall there was something that looked like an improvised cooking stove. My eyes swept the room again, and I saw a dark shadow in the corner. The light from the lamp barely reached the edges of the room, so I couldn't make out what it was until it moved. A small figure eased silently from the corner, and I realized that this was the child. She moved to Maggie's side, and I watched as Maggie's arm went automatically around the little girl's shoulders.

"Greta, these are my friends—" her voice hesitated on the word *friends*—"Mr. and Mrs. O'Connor." I turned my gaze to Jack and gave him a meaningful look. He needed to clear that up. As soon as possible.

Jack turned to the little girl, crouched down, took his hat off, and said something in rapid German. The little girl smiled but huddled in slightly to Maggie's leg.

"Greta doesn't speak," Maggie said.

Jack didn't look up, but he switched instantly back to English. "At all?"

"Not since I've known her. She understands everything we say, both in German and in English, but for some reason, she's never said a word." Maggie glanced at us, looking like she was ready to leap to the silent child's defense.

I took a step toward Greta and crouched down. "I am—" I almost said Miss Fortune but caught myself before I dropped that bombshell. "You can call me Miss Allie, and I'm very excited to meet you. Mr. O'Connor and I have come a long way to meet you." Greta smiled, clearly understanding every word, and I saw the light of curiosity flare in her eyes. Whatever caused this little girl's silence, I was fairly certain it had nothing to do with intelligence.

I took another look at Greta. I wasn't an expert on children, but if I'd had to guess I would have said that she was five or six. She was small. In height, but she was also slight, slender to the point that it looked unhealthy. I imagined there were a lot of children that looked like this in Berlin, but it still made me sad to see it.

Jack took two chocolate bars out of his overcoat pocket and handed one to Greta, then reached up and handed one to Maggie, without ever taking his eyes off the little girl. She smiled politely, but it was clear she had no idea what he'd just given her.

"Do you like chocolate?" he asked.

She shrugged and turned to Maggie for the answer.

Maggie smiled. "You will. I almost guarantee it."

Jack stretched out his hand, and Greta reluctantly put the bar back into it. He laughed, then unwrapped a section of chocolate, broke it off and handed it to her. We all watched as she put it into her mouth, closed her eyes, and savored the sweet treat. After a minute she opened her eyes and held out her hand for another chunk. We all laughed.

It seemed to release some of the tension, and I nearly sighed with relief. I bent down next to Jack and spoke softly. "Greta, why don't you show me around your home?"

I turned for a second to look at Jack, letting him know with my eyes that it was time to set Maggie straight on a few things. He apparently got the message as he rose and moved over to where Maggie stood.

Chapter 20

MAGGIE

MAGGIE FOLLOWED Jack to a corner of the room, out of hearing of the woman and child. He turned to her and she felt a hitch in her pulse as her eyes met his. He looked older, even more so than the five years apart could have accounted for. He also looked tired, bruises under his eyes a silent witness to the effort it had taken for him to get here.

Maggie swallowed over the lump in her throat. "Thank you so much for coming." He couldn't possibly understand how much it meant.

"You can stop saying that now." His words came out sharply, and Maggie felt like she'd been slapped.

He must have seen the hurt flicker across her

face. He sighed and scraped his hands across his face, muttering under his breath, "Sorry. I meant, you don't need to keep saying thank you." The words were clipped, and Maggie just nodded. "Also, you need to know Allie's not my wife."

"Who is she then?"

"She's a friend, a colleague. She helped me get here and helped me with a plan for getting all of us back out of here."

Maggie needed a moment to form her response. "Any friend willing to travel halfway across the world to help someone is a good friend indeed."

Jack nodded, and she wished for a second that she could still read his thoughts. Before, a lifetime ago, they wouldn't have needed words, but this Jack was completely closed to her. And she felt the disconnect in every fiber of her being.

"She is. She's the bravest and most loyal person I know."

Maggie felt her heart sink. For a moment, just a brief second, she'd let herself wonder about what it meant that Jack was not married, and that he'd come all this way for her. But that little flare of light sputtered out at his words. Even if they weren't married, Jack clearly thought highly of Allie. Maybe she didn't want to get married. Maybe Jack was hoping to change her mind, was trying to win her over.

Maggie forced a smile. "I'm looking forward to getting to know her."

Chapter 21

ALLIE

AS JACK AND MAGGIE moved away to talk in semiprivate, Greta reached out and grasped my hand to show me around the room. There wasn't much to see, but she was proud of what they did have and she pointed out where they ate, where they slept, and everything in between. When we'd made a circle of the room she opened a door to what must have been a bedroom at one time. It now seemed to be used for storage. Inside was a suitcase, some clothing, and a box that contained their food rations. Greta carefully stuck what was left of the chocolate bar into the box, then we headed back out to the main room. The sound of a hushed conversation broke off as we came back in. Maggie put on a bright smile, and Jack took a step away from her, his arms crossed over his chest, his expression remote.

"Have you shown our guest everything?" she asked. The little girl nodded. "Excellent. We need to get started making supper for them then. Could you help me by bringing in the food box please?"

I knew how scarce the food was here, and having seen the food box already I knew that their supplies were meager at best. "I don't need anything to eat," I said. "I'm not hungry right now."

Greta stared up at me in incomprehension, as though she couldn't imagine not being hungry.

Maggie smiled and shook her head. "You are our guests; please share what we have with us."

Torn, I didn't know what to do. The last thing I wanted to do was eat a single bite of food that could be given to that tiny child who needed it far more than I, but I also understood pride. I nodded. "Thank you."

Maggie and Greta worked together to make dumplings and set a pot of soup onto their little cookstove to boil. The soup must have been made yesterday as it only took half an hour or so to be ready.

We ate the soup and dumplings in silence, chatting a little, but mostly for Greta's benefit. It was understood that we wouldn't talk until she was asleep.

Thankfully Greta started yawning even before she was finished eating, and Jack and I tidied up from supper as Maggie went to put Greta down to sleep on the mattress in the corner. I heard her singing softly to the little girl, and I felt a little tug on my heart. Greta might not be Maggie's by birth, but there was no question, she was the little girl's mother.

Maggie got up from the mattress and crossed back to us. "Please bring the chairs into the other room.

It's a long story, and I don't want to disturb her." With that she took the hurricane lamp off of the table, and she led us, each carrying a chair, into the storage room.

We set the chairs down, and Maggie sat on top of a large box. We faced each other in silence, and I tried to tamp down my impatience to finally hear what had brought us all the way to Berlin.

Chapter 22

WE WAITED IN silence for a moment. It looked to me like Maggie was trying to figure out where to begin her tale.

"Before I start, you have to understand that things are different here. The rules of civilized society have been stripped away, trumped by the need to survive. People do things here that wouldn't be acceptable in other places, but at this time, in this place, it's just a matter of necessity."

Her words made me even more curious, but I remained silent.

"Let me give you some background information first. Greta and I found each other about a year ago. She's an orphan, both of her parents killed during the war. Her aunt looked after her for a while, but with her own four children to feed, she decided she couldn't support an extra child. She dropped Greta off at one of the orphanages in the city.

"Conditions in the orphanages are bad. Very bad. Little food, too many children, it's not pretty. Anyway, the children were often sent out to scavenge what they could, stand in ration lines, do whatever was needed. I found Greta sifting through the rubble of a house destroyed by bombers.

"Most of the destroyed buildings have already been salvaged and picked clean of everything useful, but every once in a while, if you look hard enough you can find something of value that was missed. That's what Greta was doing when I found her. Unfortunately where there's rubble, there's also danger. Unexploded ordnance, glass, sharp metal, all kinds of dangers exist for rubble pickers.

"I was walking down the street, on my way to the makeshift hospital I'd been working at, when I came across this little girl who was holding her hand and crying. I came over to her and saw that she'd cut herself on a ragged shard of glass. The cut was deep, and it stretched all the way from above her wrist to her palm. I checked it out and saw that it was bleeding heavily enough that she could have nicked an artery. I knew she needed to get it stitched quickly. So I picked her up and carried her to the hospital. By the time we got there she was unconscious. It was a good thing, as medical supplies are even scarcer than food around here and minor things like stitches are done without anesthetic."

I shuddered at the thought of feeling a needle and thread pulling skin together.

"We got her stitched up, gave her a bed to recover in, and got on with the rest of the patients that needed to be seen that day. It was only after my shift was over that I realized no one had come for her. She was still in that bed, asleep, like she hadn't had a restful sleep in a very long time. I woke her up, told her that someone would be worried about her, that she needed to get home. It took me awhile, but with the use of many hand gestures and much guessing I figured out that she was from one of the local orphanages. And it struck me that no one knew where she was, this vulnerable little girl who didn't speak. She was all on her own."

Maggie's face reflected the sadness of that statement. "I'd already seen so much awful stuff in the war and in the aftermath, but for some reason, that hit me hard. Here was this beautiful seven-year-old girl, and no one loved her enough to notice she was missing. It wasn't practical, it didn't make any sense or fit with my lifestyle in any way, but I felt like God was whispering into my soul that I was meant to look after this child. That this, she was the meaning and purpose I'd been looking for. That He'd placed us in the same city at the same time because I was meant to make sure she grew up loved."

Maggie shook her head. "I can't explain it any better than that, but for years, since the middle of the war, I'd been questioning God, wondering if my life would end up meaning anything. I walked away from everything and everyone I knew in some sort of a search for purpose." She looked at Jack as though measuring his reaction to her words. "Just to find myself in a place where I could fix broken bones and bodies all I wanted but still did not have the soul-deep purpose I was looking for. Working on a medical assembly line, patch, fix, send back out to fight again, seemed to reinforce that my search for meaning was merely chasing after the wind."

She shook her head. "And then I met Greta, and I felt like all of a sudden I understood. I'd been waiting for her. I brought her something to eat, told her to relax and go back to sleep, and then I walked to the orphanage and made arrangements to adopt Greta." She smiled. "It was eleven o'clock at night, and there I was knocking, getting the matron up out of bed, insisting that we make arrangements and do the paperwork that night."

I couldn't hold back my surprise. "And they let you? Just like that?"

Maggie smiled, but it was sad. "They're good people, doing the best they can, but honestly, she was just one more child that they didn't have enough room for. They were relieved to have another bed open up. That's how they saw her. A body taking up a bed."

Maggie was silent for a few moments. "And so

we ended up together. Everything was fine until a month ago. I was working at the hospital, and Greta was supposed to be standing in line for rations. The store where she'd been in line ran out of supplies long before she got any, so she went off to play until I got home from work. It wasn't as cold then as it is now, and there are always kids playing in the streets, kicking around a rock, pretending it's a ball. Greta went off to play for a while but instead of finding some kids to play with, she found an abandoned building to play in. She knows better than to play in abandoned buildings, but like I said, she's eight years old. Something caught her eye, and she went inside."

Maggie took a deep breath. "What she found in there is what has brought all of this trouble down on our heads."

"What did she find, Maggie?" Jack's voice was gentle.

"She found a dead Russian officer. Shot in the chest. She indicated that there was a trail of blood across the floor, so I suspect that he was shot out on the street somewhere and ducked inside the building to hide. Greta had been around enough dead bodies to know that he hadn't been dead long. She let me know that there was no smell."

I felt slightly ill to think that a child that young already knew so much about death.

"Anyway, this is Berlin. People have learned to do what they must to survive. Greta learned that lesson earlier than most." Maggie was embarrassed. I could see it in her face. "I don't approve of this, but Greta thought she was doing the right thing . . ." She trailed off.

"What did she do, Maggie?" Jack asked.

"She stripped the body." Maggie said it quickly. "Everything of value has a price on the black market. She took his boots, his gun, and even the pouch he had strapped across his chest, hidden between his shirt and his coat."

"Okay, so she took his stuff. I'm assuming that his boots and gun aren't what got you into the kind of trouble you're talking about," Jack said.

"No. It was the pouch or, more correctly, its contents, that have made Greta and me the most wanted people in all of Germany."

"In all of Germany?" I asked, skepticism clear in my voice.

Maggie nodded.

Jack straightened, his eyes hard. "What was in the pouch?"

Maggie bit her lip. "I can't tell you."

"You have to, Maggie, or we can't help you," I said.

"You don't understand. Not knowing what I know might actually save your life."

"What do you mean?"

"If you don't know anything, then the people who will kill for this information will have no interest in you. It's better if all you know is that

Greta found something, papers that have information that could get a lot of people killed if they got into the wrong hands."

Jack nodded. "Okay, then what about getting them into the right hands?"

"I've already tried that. It ended up with two men dead, me branded as a murderer, and now the British, the American, and the Soviet governments have a description of me, and they are all scouring the city to find me. And I have my doubts that any of those governments care very much if me or Greta end up dead too, as long as they are the ones to find those documents first."

Jack was silent several seconds. "Your passport?" he asked.

"Useless. I'll never get across the border alive using it. They know my name."

Jack swore under his breath. "You're sure?"

"Positive. There's also a sketch that looks pretty similar to me with my name on it at every border crossing in Germany. I am not exaggerating when I say that half of this city is on the lookout for me. I have a few friends, whom I trust completely, that have kept an eye on the situation for me. Other than to go to the airfield every day to see if you've come, Greta and I haven't been out of this apartment for two weeks. We had to leave our home in the American sector, leave all of our possessions behind. We came here because the French sector is the least organized and the least patrolled. We're running out of food, and we can't buy any, because there are soldiers patrolling all over the city, waiting for one of us to line up somewhere."

"Greta can't line up either?" I asked.

"We have to use ID to get a ration card, and a ration card to get food, so no, she can't do it either."

"Okay, let me see if I have the facts straight. You know something and have proof of something that the Americans, the British, and the Soviets want desperately. They're searching for you and Greta because they think you murdered someone, and if you try to use your passport to get out of the city, they're going to catch you." Jack shoved himself out of the chair and began to pace as he spoke. "Does that about sum it up?" he asked.

"They actually think I murdered two American soldiers, but that's the big picture, yes," Maggie said.

Jack stared at her for a second and then started to pace again. "Who killed the men you supposedly murdered?"

"I have no idea, but I'm fairly sure they were after me and Greta."

"You have to tell us more—what happened, how you ended up in this mess." Jack's words came out frustrated and sharp.

She shook her head. "I can't. I need you to trust me. The more you know, the more danger you're in, and I've already put you in harm's way by asking you to come. Please just trust me." There seemed to be more to her words, a meaning that was just for Jack. I saw him nod. After a moment of tense silence I brought us back around to the practical.

"So we need to find a way to get you out of Berlin without a passport, without being seen," I said.

"Both of us. I'm not going anywhere without Greta." Her voice was sharp.

"Of course." I nodded. "That's a given."

Maggie nodded too. "It's not an exaggeration to say that if we don't get out of here soon, both of us are going to end up dead." There was absolute certainty in Maggie's voice. "We're running out of supplies, and we can't hide much longer."

Chapter 23

MAGGIE

"OKAY, GIVE ALLIE and me some time to think about this. I'm sure there's a way to get both of you out."

Maggie smiled wearily at his optimism. "I understand. This is a lot of information to be dropped on you all at once. You'll need some time to think it over." There was a moment of silence before Maggie asked the question that had been nagging.

She looked from Jack to Allie. "Jack tells me that I jumped to the wrong conclusion—that you two aren't really married."

"We're not. We used that as a cover to get here, but we're just partners," Allie said, when it appeared that Jack wasn't going to answer.

"You're FBI?" Maggie asked, voice full of doubt.

"No. I'm a private investigator and a good friend of Jack's. We've worked together before, and when he told me about the trouble you were in, I offered to come over and help get you out."

Maggie felt her eyes narrow, but she didn't say any more. How good of friends did you have to be to cross the world and risk your life for a friend of your friend? She couldn't help but wonder.

Allie gave her a look, as though she knew exactly what Maggie was thinking. At that point Maggie decided it was time to wrap things up for the night. She crossed to the box where she'd set the lamp, the only source of illumination in the room. "I'll let you two figure out the sleeping arrangements for tonight, and then we should all get some rest."

"I'll sleep on the floor in here," Jack offered.

"Okay, I'll find a spot in the other room with Maggie and Greta then," Allie said. Maggie gave Jack a moment to find a spot and sit down before she opened the door and led the way to the other room.

• • •

As she set out to make Allie and Jack as comfortable as possible in this makeshift home, Maggie's thoughts drifted back to the last time she'd seen him.

SEPTEMBER 1940

The moment was at hand. Maggie forced her smile not to waver as the minister said the words. Man and wife.

The lace at her throat felt constricting and scratchy, and she tried not to fidget. Surrounded by flowers and white silk she thought for a moment she was going to suffocate. She tried to subtly move the bouquet of gardenias in her hands farther away from her face. The fragrance was still overwhelming but slightly more tolerable. Drawing in a deep breath she looked to her left.

At the edge of her peripheral vision she saw Jack, dashing in his tux, beaming at the happy couple. Instantly she realized she'd let her mind wander, and she cranked up her smile to brilliant. Jack sent her a lightning-quick questioning glance, but she was fairly sure he was the only one who could detect the hint of something forced in her expression.

Richard was a nice man, and he seemed to genuinely love Dinah, but it seemed to Maggie that something was missing. Like any spark of personality. The unkind thought made Maggie wince with guilt. It was just hard to understand what Dinah saw in him. He was nothing like the ideal man they'd dreamed and giggled about for years. Richard had a small but successful dental practice, but was having a comfortable life with a boring man really going to be enough for Dinah?

What had happened to all of Dinah's dreams of adventure and romance? Richard's bad back and lack of imagination made it highly unlikely he'd ever sweep her off her feet literally or figuratively. For the life of her Maggie couldn't understand the attraction. Still, if Richard was what Dinah wanted, then Maggie was happy for her.

Maggie turned to watch the happy couple walk back down the aisle, this time as husband and wife. Dinah looked blissful.

After a moment Maggie turned to Jack, who was standing on the other side of the aisle in the space reserved for groomsmen. He held out his elbow to her, and she took a step toward him, then threaded her arm through his and they made their slow progress out of the church.

"You okay?" Jack whispered, keeping his eyes straight ahead.

"Fine." She drew strength from the reassuring squeeze of his arm. She could always count on Jack; he never let her down, and he always seemed to understand how she was feeling—often before she did.

Knowing that there were still wedding party photos

to take and then the reception and dinner to get through, she was going to need all the strength she could get.

"Save me a dance?" Jack asked under his breath. "One?"

He turned and sent her a grin so dazzling she had to stifle a laugh. "All of them."

This time she couldn't fight the laugh that wanted to escape. "Done," she said, her smile not feeling forced for the first time all day.

The meal finally ended, and the band started to play, a brassy big band sound. Considering they only had five band members, they were pretty good. They played recognizable versions of Tommy Dorsey songs, and it seemed that the lead singer thought he was going to be the next Frank Sinatra. He was good, but he wasn't going to be challenging the rising star anytime soon.

The hall for the reception was packed with friends and family of both sides, and the mood was exuberant. Dinah flitted from table to table talking to everyone, clearly delighted to be the center of attention. It made Maggie smile.

The music swelled around her and filled her with a new reserve of energy. She gently patted at her hair, all too aware that the humidity would have her soft red-gold curls springing loose of her carefully arranged hairstyle.

A tap on her shoulder brought her out of her

thoughts. Jack leaned over her shoulder and smiled. "Ready for that dance you promised?" he asked.

Being near him brought the same soft flush of happiness that it always did, and she wondered how she ever would have made it to adulthood without him. Her best friend, protector, and biggest encourager since she was fifteen years old, he'd never once let her down.

For the past year he'd been away a lot, coming home a few weekends a month, and she'd missed him more than she had imagined she would. Still, getting into the FBI was his dream, and she felt a rush of pride at how close he was to achieving it. And he'd pushed her, hard at times, to achieve her dreams too. Nursing school hadn't been easy, but graduating last spring had been one of the most momentous days of her life.

He'd been there for that too, beaming with pride, making up with his enthusiasm for the fact that she had no real family to congratulate her on her success.

Maggie let Jack lead her out onto the crowded dance floor, smiling at how easy everything was for him. Crowds parted, people turned to look when Jack walked by. Maggie knew she didn't draw the same attention. With her soft grey eyes, red-gold hair, and reserved smile people's gazes often skipped over her when she stood next to him, but she didn't mind. She had no desire to be the center of attention.

Jack drew her into his arms, and she fell into rhythm with his steps immediately. Dancing, like everything else, was easy for Jack, and he led her smoothly across the room. Relaxed for the first time all day, Maggie looked up at him and grinned. He was just so . . . Jack.

No words were needed. Completely at ease in his arms, Maggie let her mind drift as the band changed songs and they just kept dancing. Finally, after yet another song ended, Jack pulled back a fraction, and Maggie smiled wearily up at him.

"Why don't we go outside for a little fresh air?" He released her, took a step back, and put his hands in his pockets.

Feeling content and a little tired, she just nodded and followed as Jack led her to the hall's side door, threading them through the crowd with ease.

Once outside Maggie was surprised to see that the moon was high overhead and the sun had long since set. The cool fall air felt so good after the stifling heat of the hall. She moved out into the open and let the breeze surround her.

Feeling deliciously relaxed and happy, she turned back to Jack. "All in all, it was a good day."

Lit by moonlight, Jack's expression was unreadable. "It was."

"Dinah seems happy." A strange feeling rippled through her at Jack's serious expression. "I'm so glad you were able to get the weekend off and be here today. It seems like the FBI has been keeping you away from home more and more these days. I've missed you." She had to fight the urge to babble.

"Have you really missed me, Maggie?" he asked. Something heavy in his voice gave her pause.

"You know I have. You're my very best friend. I always miss you when you're gone."

"But the question is, do you miss me only as your old friend, or something more? Do you miss me the way I miss you when I'm gone? Where I'm counting the days until I get to see you again? When all I can think about is coming back here and seeing you smile at me?"

"Jack—" She wanted to stop him, was desperate to keep whatever it was he was trying to tell her from being said.

He moved a step closer and reached out and placed his hands around her arms, loosely holding her to him, forcing her to meet his gaze.

"I love you, Maggie. I want to be your best friend, your husband, and your lover more than I want any-thing else in the world." She made a sound, tried to interrupt, but he kept talking. "I can't wait anymore, it seems like I've already been waiting forever. I need you to marry me. Please, Maggie, will you marry me?"

Waves of hot and cold ran through her. She took a step back, out of his reach, and circled her arms around herself. "Jack—." Tears threatened, and she had to fight them back for a moment before she could speak.

"Jack, you know I love you, you're the most important person in my life, but I can't do what you're asking me to do." The words ended on a choked sob. "I can't get married, not to you or anyone. I'm not ready, I don't know if I'll ever be ready." With each word she knew she was destroying their relationship. She could see from the look on his face that she was breaking something inside him, and she could feel an echo of it breaking in her too. She shook her head. "I'm sorry, I can't." She turned away, unable to witness the effect of her words on the best man she'd ever known.

Chapter 24

ALLIE

THE NIGHT FELT endless. I had never experienced such suffocating darkness before. I'd known long before Maggie had blown out the lamp that I wouldn't be able to sleep, but spending an entire night sitting with my back pressed up against the wall, in darkness so complete it made me dizzy, made me realize that insomnia was much worse when it was in combination with total blackness. I longed for the familiar night noises of New York.

I tried to keep my mind occupied with thoughts of my mother and her mysterious box. I'd taken a closer look at it on the drive from France, and something about it intrigued me. It was beautiful, the inlaid wood so intricate that the design on top looked like it had been painted on.

I couldn't imagine who my mother would know in Berlin, never mind be desperate enough to get into contact with, that she would be willing to make a deal with me for my services.

I knew we had relatives in France and Belgium, and that my parents had many friends in Britain, but I'd never heard my mother speak about anyone she knew in Berlin. It was all very confusing. I wanted to chalk it up to my mother being deliberately mysterious, but something in her eyes when she'd been in my office had told me that she hadn't really been playing our usual game. There'd been something serious in her when she'd asked me to do this.

A priest, a beautiful wooden piece of art, and my mother acknowledging that I am a private detective, never mind procuring my services. Something strange was going on.

I shoved the thoughts aside and tried to calculate how long it might be before morning.

I heard rather than saw dawn breaking. I could hear it in Greta and Maggie's restless movements. Their bodies told them that it would be time to rise soon. I heard Maggie mutter in her sleep and felt a flush of embarrassment when I heard her call out Jack's name. The unconscious workings of her mind were private, and I felt guilty for overhearing her when she was defenseless. But in a way it reassured me that she still had some sort of attachment to Jack. She'd been so hard to read yesterday. I hadn't been able to see what she was thinking.

Was she simply happy to see Jack because he was there to help her, or was there more? I hurt for him. I knew how he felt. Despite the total lack of emotion he'd shown for most of yesterday, I knew that he was still in love with Maggie. Through the long night I had to wonder, though, if he loved *this* Maggie, or if he was still in love with the Maggie of his past. Because *this* Maggie had served at the front lines of a war, had seen and done things that I was sure had changed her. I wondered if Jack really even knew her anymore.

It didn't escape my notice that if I ever saw David again, those same questions would probably apply to me. Do people really change, at their core? Do their experiences make them different people? I had no answers, and I tried to shove the thoughts aside as I waited for a new day to dawn.

The sound of Maggie rising from her bed, moving stealthily, brought a sense of relief. "Good morning." The words were barely a whisper, but I heard her turn toward me and wondered if I'd scared her.

"Morning, Allie," she said after a moment. She stepped in my direction but stopped when she was still several feet away. I heard the scrape of a match, and the flare of light brought with it my first easy breath in hours. She touched the flame to the wick and within seconds the room lit up. What had seemed dim last night now felt like the lights they used to illuminate the stages of Broadway.

"How did you sleep?" she asked. Her red-gold hair was rumpled, but there didn't seem to be any tiredness lingering on her face.

I didn't know what to say. I didn't want to lie. "About the same as usual." There. It was the truth.

Maggie's eyes narrowed, and she dismissed my hedging answer. She took a long look at me, assessing me for herself. After several long moments she turned away to pull the blanket back up over Greta's shoulders. Only when her back was to me did she speak. "So do you normally have trouble sleeping, or is this something new?"

"It's been going on for a long time." I didn't bother avoiding the direct question.

"I knew a nurse once, I worked with her when I was in Africa, and she could only sleep for an hour at a time. She kept a journal and a lamp next to her bed, and in all of the hours she spent awake when she should have been sleeping, she would write. Anything, everything. About her experiences, short stories. Sometimes she'd write letters home for the soldiers she treated. It seemed to help her pass the time." The words were casual, but I felt my jaw drop open. Other than my doctor,

I'd never actually heard of anyone else who had the same problems I did.

"I work on cases." The words slipped out. I wasn't even sure I liked this woman. I hadn't intended on getting into a personal conversation with her. "I just stay at my office and write up reports, mull over cases, and if things are really bad, I balance my books."

Maggie smiled a little. "I guess you just have to learn to cope with it."

I nodded.

Emboldened by our little moment of understanding I took a risk. "Are you glad to see Jack?" I asked. "For reasons beyond the help you've asked for?"

Maggie stopped the rummaging she'd been doing in the food bin, pushed herself up, and faced me. She regarded me in complete stillness for a moment. "Would it bother you if I was?" She turned the question back to me.

I thought my words out carefully before releasing them. "In a way. But not in the way you think. I'm not in love with Jack. I sort of wish I was. I'm just worried. I know that this situation . . ." I stopped, corrected myself. ". . . that you have the power to hurt him. And that does bother me."

"And you want to know if I want him back, or if I just want him to save me."

I nodded. "Yeah, I do."

"Well, let me be just as blunt. That's something

that's between Jack and me." She took a deep breath. "But I can see that you're trying to protect him, so I'll tell you this much. I've known Jack most of my life, and he's always been the one person who really mattered to me. My life took a dramatic left turn, and I left New York and Jack, but I still cared about him. I don't know about now, and I doubt Jack does either. So the honest truth is, I can't answer that question. And really, Jack's happiness or my own are very much secondary considerations at the moment." She glanced toward the bed. "Greta is the most important thing in my life, and her happiness and her safety come first. We'll deal with everything else later."

I believed her and maybe respected her a little for her honesty. We were both silent for a few minutes. "What do we do today?" I asked.

Maggie opened her mouth to speak, but we both turned at the sound of a door opening behind us. Jack stepped out of the other room, a little rumpled and a little grumpy looking. I wondered for a second if he'd heard our conversation, but I pushed the thought from my mind.

"Morning," he mumbled, scraping his hands over his face.

Maggie just nodded, and I sent him a smile. I wasn't sure how things were going to work out for these two, but I was sure of one thing. No matter what it took, we were going to get out of Berlin and give them both a chance to find out.

Chapter 25

MAGGIE, JACK, AND I talked quietly, not wanting to wake Greta. Maggie mixed a little flour with some water and went about making breakfast for herself and Greta. Both Jack and I had declined, claiming we weren't hungry.

"I didn't want to get into this discussion last night, but how did you two manage to get into Berlin? It must have taken some doing." Maggie turned back to us, her hands dusted with flour and a white streak crossing her face from forehead to cheekbone. Her grey eyes were serious, and despite everything she looked beautiful. It made me wonder how much more so she'd look if she laughed. I wondered how long it had been since she'd felt free, had laughed because she was happy. I had the feeling it'd been awhile.

I let Jack answer. "There's a program back home that allows various charitable organizations to bring back groups of German orphans to be adopted into American families. We have papers saying that we are from such a group and that we will be leaving this country in a week or so with eight children to be taken to the United States."

Maggie's face lit up. "That's amazing. You could get Greta out no problem." She was silent for several moments, and I knew she was thinking what both of us had already realized. It wasn't going to be hard to get Greta out, but Maggie was a different story entirely. Even if every border guard hadn't been on the lookout for her, we still had no legitimate reason to take another adult with us when we left Berlin. That left us illegitimate reasons. And those were far riskier.

"We'll have to come up with the rest of the plan as we go, but for right now, we've got a good start." Jack's voice was cheerful, to my ears desperately so. I smiled and tried to feign confidence I didn't have.

"I'm sure we can come up with something. We've got a few days." I took a deep breath. "And that brings us back to today. What do we need to do right now?"

Maggie was the first to speak. "I can't come out with you during the day, but if we can work after dark as well, I can help out tonight."

I nodded. Jack turned to me. "One thing that we must do is get the supplies that we left in the car and bring them back here." It would probably take several trips, but it was just too risky to leave all of our bartering tools in the untended vehicle.

"It would be a good thing to do a better job at hiding it too," Maggie added.

"And then we need to get on with our cover reason for being here," Jack said. "It will seem suspicious if we aren't making the rounds of the local orphanages when that's why we're here." He paused. "Maggie, I know you feel that it's best not to tell us what you found, but I do have a couple of questions about it that I think you need to answer.

"First off, if we needed to leave on short notice, how long would it take you to access the pouch?"

She thought for a second. "A little over an hour I'd guess."

"What are you going to do with it once we get it out of Berlin?" His voice was deceptively soft.

Maggie's answer was instant. "Once I'm safely out, I'll hand it over to you, and you can hand it over to whichever American authorities need to see it."

Jack nodded, and I saw his whole body relax. "Okay. Allie and I are going to walk back to the car and start unloading supplies."

"What all have you brought?" she asked, biting her lip.

"There are two jerry cans of gasoline in the trunk, four cases of chocolate bars, and our clothes and personal items."

She shook her head. "If anyone knew what you had in there, that car would be stripped and looted faster than you could walk back there. If only you'd brought some flour and coffee, you could sell it all on the black market and set yourself up as king of Berlin." She grinned as she spoke, and I saw that I was right. She was breathtaking when she smiled. Not beautiful so much as vivid and alive. I felt a twinge of envy when I caught the answering smile on Jack's face, but I tamped it down. I only wanted the best for Jack, and while I still wasn't sure that was Maggie, I knew for sure it wasn't me. I had to force those feelings aside and focus on the tasks at hand.

"Okay, let's go empty the car, get the lay of the land, and then we'll set out for the closest orphanage."

Jack ripped his eyes from Maggie's, and I realized that while I'd been swallowing my jealousy, they'd been having a moment, one of those looks that neither of them could turn away from. I turned away, picked up my coat, shrugged it on, and headed for the door.

I heard Jack following a few footsteps behind, but didn't turn, just walked out into the frozen air of pre-dawn Berlin.

Chapter 26

MAGGIE

MAGGIE WATCHED them leave with a clutch of fear in her heart. Fear that they would be seen, that something would happen to them, that they wouldn't come back. She forced herself to concentrate on the fact that they were here and that they'd come to help.

Allie seemed very efficient and logical. And beautiful. Maggie imagined that she was probably an excellent private investigator, and Jack, well,

Jack had worked for the FBI for years. His experience was going to be invaluable in getting out of Berlin.

Keeping an eye on Greta, Maggie rose and moved to start the daily chores that made this apartment feel a little more like home and that kept her from losing her mind at the enforced isolation. Her thoughts, without prodding, slid to the past.

OCTOBER 1941

It had been a week since she'd hurt her best friend and destroyed the most important part of her life. It had been a week of misery and life-changing decisions. She couldn't stay, couldn't see Jack and pretend things were as they had been. His question, his words had changed everything and there was no going back.

She hadn't felt so alone since the hideous weeks after her parents' deaths.

Wishing things were different, that her feelings were different, didn't change anything, and just today she'd realized she couldn't stay here anymore. Not in this house and not in New York. It was time to go, time to get out into the world and do the things she needed to do. Time to find out who Margaret Katherine O'Shayne really was. Was she simply that orphan girl the Marculis had taken in, or was she something, someone more? Someone her mother and father would have been proud of?

She picked up the stack of paperwork that lay on her bedspread and read it over again, hardly able to believe that she'd actually done it. She'd enlisted in the Army medical corps. She'd been told to report to a military hospital in Virginia in a week for training.

Jack was going to be furious. She squashed the thought almost as soon as it appeared in her mind, but not soon enough to prevent the battering ache in her chest when she thought of him. If only things could have been different, if only she could have been the woman he needed. More than anything, she wished she could have just said yes to Jack's proposal. But something inside her, something way down deep, told her that she wasn't enough, didn't have enough to make him truly happy.

Forcing back the thoughts that had circled ceaselessly in her mind for days, she laid the military paperwork back down and picked up the other item on the bed. A sealed envelope. Addressed to Jack.

She'd written it earlier today but had yet to find the courage to actually mail it. It was the final step, the final blow that would sever the only real tie she had in her life. Jack had been her anchor for so many years, and she felt lost and adrift at the realization that she was now completely alone in the world.

Fingering the letter she remembered how hard it had been to find the words.

Jack,

I apologize for not having the courage to do this in person. I have discovered in the past week that I am a coward, a humbling realization. I need to tell you, even if only on paper, how sorry I am for the way things ended on Saturday. I never wanted to, meant to hurt you like that. How pathetic my excuses look in black and white. I have no words to make things better or to fix anything. I can only say I'm sorry. And tell you that I have to leave. I can't stay here and pretend that things are all right. I think in the long run it will be best for both of us.

You have been my best friend, my support, my everything for so long, and now that that's gone I can't help but wonder what's left of me. Who am I, what am I meant to do with my life? All I know is that the answers don't lie here, I can't be tested if I never leave my cocoon of safety.

I have enlisted in the Army medical corps. They're desperate for nurses right now, what with all that's going on in Europe and I need to go.

Take care Jack and be safe,
Maggie

It sounded as pathetic now as it had then, but Maggie knew she had to mail it in order to close this part of her life. Shoving her feet into shoes, she smoothed the envelope once more between her hands before forcing herself out of the bedroom. The nearest public mailbox was only a few blocks away, but the walk seemed to take forever. Finally she slipped the letter in the metal slot. The clang of the mail drawer closing rang with sickening finality. She stared at the mailbox for a long moment before turning around and going back the way she'd come.

The next five weeks were the longest of Maggie's life. Telling her adopted family she was leaving, packing, arriving in Virginia to discover that despite everything she knew about nursing, she was walking into a completely different world with the military. Still the basic training drills and pack marches had kept her busy and exhausted. Almost exhausted enough not to think.

The letter she'd received at roll call this morning still burned in her pocket. She'd recognized the writing immediately, but to this point had been unable to open it. Ensconced in the so-called privacy of her barracks-style room, she finally felt ready to open it. Nerves fluttered through her stomach, pulse pounded slightly too hard in her throat, but she took a deep breath and did her best to control her reactions. Tearing the flap open she pulled out the letter. There were only a few lines on the single sheet.

Be safe Maggie. If you ever change your mind, I'll be here.

Always,
Jack

Chapter 27

ALLIE

THE SKY WAS lightening from charcoal to pewter, with the sun still just a promise. I huddled further into my jacket and bent my head to keep the wind off my face. Jack tromped along behind me in silence.

A few people were out already, but not many yet. Everyone we did see had the same tired look of grim determination as they went about their day.

The two miles or so back to the car seemed more like five, and by the time we reached the copse of trees where it was parked I felt frozen right through. Jack unlocked the passenger door and motioned for me to get in. I did with relief, glad to be out of the slight wind, even if the interior of the car was just as cold as the outside. He rounded to the other side, unlocked his own door, and slid in beside me. He wasted no time starting the car, and we sat in silence while the heater chugged to life.

"Any thoughts where we should hide this

thing?" I asked after I'd warmed up enough to be able to feel my fingers and toes again.

"Maggie said that the hangar at the back of the airstrip is pretty much abandoned, so we could park behind it, and no one would really want to mess with any vehicles there because they would assume that they belong to the French military."

"And the French military?"

"The hope would be that they either don't notice it, or they assume that it has a reason for being there. It's probably the safest place to leave it."

I shrugged. It wasn't a foolproof plan, but it was probably the best we were going to come up with.

He pulled the car out of the brush and drove it around behind the airplane hangar.

It only took a few hundred yards for the boxes I was carrying to start getting heavy. Jack carried the two jerry cans, and I knew they were a lot heavier and a lot more awkward than what I was toting, so I bit my lip to keep from complaining. As we walked through the streets on our way back we drew more attention this time. In the proper light of day there was a stark contrast between Jack and I and the people of Berlin. Our coats both looked new, at least in comparison with the dull, much-patched ones of the people around us, and we were carrying both gasoline and boxes with the words Hershey on the sides. After a mile the cold was no longer a problem, as carrying the boxes had helped me get warm, but my fingers were going numb, and I didn't want to have to pick up all of those chocolate bars if I ended up dropping the boxes into the snow.

"Hey, can we stop here for a minute?" I called out to Jack's back. He didn't appear to be having any trouble with the heavy cans, but he turned to me immediately. "Let's just get off the main bit of road first."

He led me a few yards off the center of the road to a section of relatively undamaged sidewalk. I set the boxes down on the ground, and Jack placed the cans down next to him. I wanted to kick him for not even being out of breath. I felt like I'd been hefting those boxes for miles.

"I've been meaning to tell you that I have a small job to do for a client while I'm here." I hadn't told Jack about my mother hiring me.

He looked at me strangely. "You have a client, other than me, who needs something done in Berlin? Really?"

"Strange, I know, but true. I'm hoping it won't take me more than an afternoon to accomplish." I felt a strange reluctance to tell Jack that my own mother had hired me. It seemed odd even in the context of my family.

"What is it?" he asked.

"Well, I'm not 100 percent sure actually. I'm supposed to try and find someone. Someone that my client hasn't actually seen since the beginning

138

of the war. I'm supposed to try and find them, or find out what happened to them."

"You going to need help?" he asked.

I laughed. "No. I think I can handle this one on my own, and besides, you're going to have your hands full with Maggie and Greta."

I took a quick look around me and saw that no one was paying us too much attention. "So, any thoughts about Maggie and her situation?" I left it deliberately vague so that if someone was listening, I wasn't really saying anything and so that if Jack misunderstood me, he could still be answering a question I was curious about: his thoughts about seeing Maggie again.

He took a look around before speaking. "No. Not really. I'll have to give it some more time. But as of right now, I think we're just going to have to take things as they come."

I fought the urge to glare. If there was one thing I hated, it was taking things as they came. I was a planner. Even if things didn't go according to plan, I still would always rather try to come up with a plan B than wing a plan A.

"Are you absolutely certain that she is innocent of what the Americans think she did?" I hated to ask, but it was necessary.

"Positive," he said shortly. I nodded.

"I think I can make it the rest of the way now." My arms were still tired, but I was starting to get cold, so it was time to get moving again.

I leaned down to pick up the boxes. When I stood up, two men in uniform stood less than two feet in front of us.

I had to fight to keep from dropping the boxes in surprise.

"Qu'est-ce que vous faites?" The words were barked at us. *"Arrêtez. Maintenent."* I stopped moving just as they said. Jack did too.

"Qu'est-ce que tu fait?" The officer on the left asked us again what we were doing.

"We're just bringing supplies to a friend," I said in French. Jack raised his eyebrow at me, probably wondering what I was saying, but I just widened my eyes slightly, communicating to him that he needed to trust me.

The officer looked suspiciously at our boxes. *"C'est quoi, ca?"* He was asking what we had.

"Nous avons un peu du chocolat." I figured it wasn't totally a lie. Perhaps someone would think that a few cases of chocolate was just a little bit.

The man narrowed his eyes at me suspiciously, then reached out and grabbed one of the boxes out of my hands. He ripped it open, revealing stacks upon stacks of chocolate bars. His eyes widened. *"Un peu?"* His look of incredulity at what I had described as a little bit of chocolate was almost comical.

Jack, who'd been silent up until now, took a step forward. "Do you speak English?" he asked, speaking loudly and slowly.

The officer nodded. *"Oui."*

I took a small step back and let Jack take over the reins of this conversation. "We're just bringing supplies to the local orphanages."

The man looked puzzled. *"Orphelinat,"* I translated.

"Ah," he said, and almost immediately his expression was a little less antagonistic. "There are many of those in Berlin," he said in heavily accented English.

Jack reached into the opened box and pulled out a handful of bars, which he offered to both officers. They reached for them eagerly.

"We are here to take a group of orphans to America," Jack explained, as the two men tore into their chocolate like excited children.

The officer who'd done most of the speaking turned his gaze back to Jack after he'd taken a bite. "You must be careful. This city is not friendly to strangers. Especially not now," he said, before taking another bite.

"What do you mean, especially not now?" Jack asked.

The French officer shook his head. "I cannot discuss it. Except to say that every sector is on high alert, looking for an American woman." He took a closer look at me, then shook his head.

"Not her. This woman has red hair."

Apparently these men hadn't heard of hair dye, but I figured that was probably a good thing.

"Why is everyone searching for an American woman?" Jack asked.

The officer shook his head. "I cannot discuss it. But security is tight. We've been given orders to detain the woman, but I know the Russians have been given 'capture by any means' orders. *Vivant ou more*," he said with a shrug.

"Dead or alive," I mouthed to Jack.

"Who is this woman and what has she done?" he asked.

The Frenchman shook his head dramatically. "Non, I cannot say any more." He straightened his shoulders. "Except to tell you that this woman has some sort of document, and she has killed two men who tried to get it from her. I know no more than this."

"Well, I can see that it would be impossible for you to answer my questions," Jack said without even the slightest hint of sarcasm staining his words. It took everything I had to keep my expression impassive. "Thank you for your time," he said, as though he were the one to have stopped them for information.

The two men straightened, nodded to both of us, and then turned and continued walking down the street.

We picked up our packages and continued on our way. We were close to Maggie's apartment before either of us spoke.

"It's as bad as she said it was," Jack commented.

"And you're surprised?" I asked.

"A little." He turned to me. "You aren't?"

I shook my head. "I saw her face. She's terrified, and I have the feeling that she doesn't scare easily."

Chapter 28

MAGGIE

THE WAITING WAS killing her. She'd done everything she could to keep Greta entertained, she'd done all of the housework she could think of, and still they weren't back. She wanted to pace but forced herself to stay still. Of its own accord her mind wandered back to the huge shift her life had taken in the dark days after Jack's proposal.

JANUARY 1941

North Africa. She'd been at the Stateside hospital for three months before she got her deployment orders. Algeria. There were no more details than that, for security reasons, but it was a relief to finally have a destination. Most of the others who'd come and gone before her were being sent to England, or undisclosed locations in the South Pacific, and being posted in Africa had never even occurred to her.

They were still two days away from boarding the ship that would take them to the other side of the

143

world, but she started packing up her belongings. After months of drifting she was relieved to finally have a purpose, a cause.

Crossing the Atlantic in a convoy of ships almost two hundred strong, her boat stuck to main shipping lanes. Once darkness fell, all of the ships maintained a total blackout. The biggest fears were German submarines or planes crossing their paths. It took eleven days to reach Africa. An evac hospital was already set up on the coast of Algeria, and six nurses were coming in to help ease the workload for the sixty or so members of the hospital staff. Fighting was fierce, and they'd been running the hospital by working twelve-hour shifts with no days off, for months.

The day she arrived Maggie and the others were herded into some sort of an office and given a quick briefing by the commanding officer of the hospital, Lt. Col. Richard Beeman. "This might not be the front lines of the war, but there is more than enough medical work for a hospital twice our size. We're situated in no-man's land here, and Rommel's forces and our boys are fighting over territory, access to oil, and just about everything else. Our boys are here to make sure that Hitler isn't going to try and appoint himself Pharaoh too. If that weren't enough, we're also being shipped wounded soldiers from Italy. They're being brought over by hospital ship.

"It's ugly. There are too many soldiers dying, and we're running at about 150 percent capacity. You'll be asked to work harder than you ever have in your life, you'll have virtually no time off, and you'll see things that I can only hope we'll all be able to forget one day."

"Wow. I think there's a future for him in recruiting," Lizzie, one of the other nurses, said under her breath.

The colonel overheard and smiled, but only slightly. "I'm not going to feed you a bunch of lies; I'm trying to prepare you for the reality of your new life."

The smile on Lizzie's face died, and Maggie felt a tightening in her gut at the man's words. Still, this was what she'd wanted. No, needed. To stop being "that poor O'Shayne girl." To stand alone and find out if she had any strength, any courage in her. Since the day she'd lost her parents she'd been dependent on the generosity of others, at the whim of others, a passive force in her own life. Over the months of waiting for orders it had become clear to Maggie why she'd had to say no to Jack and why she'd had to walk away from her entire life. He was her knight on a white horse, always there when she needed him, always ready to come to her rescue, a fairytale prince come to life. But what happened after the rescue? When the prince finally got the princess down from the tower? What happened after that? Did she have courage, strength of character? Was she kind, would she stand up against injustice? Or was she simply a blank slate, nothing more or less than what the prince thought she was?

She hoped that Africa might be the place where she could begin the process of finding out.

The lieutenant colonel concluded his welcome-to-the-combat-zone speech and took them on a quick tour of the hospital. The newcomers were joining the staff of an already formed hospital. Most of the doctors, nurses, and hospital personnel had trained together in the States before being shipped over to Algeria as a complete unit. Unfortunately, due to unexpectedly high volumes of patients, they'd had to put in a request for more nurses. That was where they came in.

They'd be working at an evac hospital. An evac did emergency surgeries and stabilizations. Similar to what an emergency ward did Stateside.

Three years of nursing school had done nothing to prepare Maggie for the reality of battlefield medicine. There were patients everywhere, surgeries going on in what basically amounted to a tent, with sterile fields made up of sheets pinned to the roof. Tents full of soldiers either recovering or waiting to be transferred to another hospital. Colonel Beeman explained that this mobile hospital was the best hope for the seriously wounded, and thus it had one of the best survival rates in the entire military.

She watched as the on-duty nurses moved from patient to patient, checking charts, checking vitals, squeezing wounded boys' hands. The combination of efficiency and compassion spoke to her.

She felt tears fill her eyes at the seemingly endless rows of patients, all seriously injured if they were here, each one of them with a life, a family, a story that went beyond just being a soldier who had lost a leg or an arm or an eye in the war.

"Whoa," Lizzie muttered under her breath.

Maggie couldn't speak past the lump in her throat, but just nodded.

"It's starting to seem real now, isn't it?" Lizzie said, soft enough that only Maggie could hear.

"Too real," she said, then followed behind the lieutenant colonel as he started walking again and showed them to the nurses' quarters. She and Lizzie claimed a room together and began unpacking their few belongings.

Maggie lay down on the stiff canvas cot and closed her eyes. She'd started out on this journey to discover who she really was, and it looked like she was going to get her wish. A trial by fire.

The sound of Jack and Allie returning yanked Maggie from her thoughts, and she went to greet them. As she turned the doorknob to let them in she said a quick prayer of thanks for their safe return.

Chapter 29

ALLIE

GRETA WAS UP BY the time Jack and I finally got back. I was fairly sure my arms would ache for days, but at least we had our supplies.

Jack and Maggie stood in the corner, discussing our run-in with the French soldiers, I assumed. I let the silent little girl show me where to put all of the things we'd brought with us. Maggie came over to me. "Jack has told me that you both need to go to an orphanage today to keep up with your official reason for being in Berlin."

I nodded. "We do."

Maggie nodded. "I can give you directions to one a few miles away. Greta and I will stay here, obviously, but tonight, after dark, I will be able to go out without putting any of us into too much danger."

I didn't comment at the use of the qualifier too much.

"If you're sure it's safe," I said, knowing that she was far more familiar with what was dangerous in this place and what wasn't.

"I've heard rumors of a rather large movement of troops out of the city in the American sector. It's to take place in two or three days, and I thought it might be of some help with our escape.

I'd like to go out and investigate the rumors myself. Talk to a friend, find out a little more."

I had the distinct feeling there was more she wanted to say but was holding back. I waited.

"I'd like to take Jack with me. Could you stay here with Greta?" she asked, looking uncomfortable at having to ask.

I considered it for a moment. I didn't want to be left behind, but I also understood that someone had to stay with Greta. I gritted my teeth, then forced myself to answer, "Yes, I'll stay behind tonight."

Maggie's face relaxed instantly. "Thank you."

I wouldn't let my face twist into a scowl, even though I was beyond frustrated. "Just find a way for all of us to get out of here, and we'll call it even."

"It's my only priority," she promised.

Jack and I walked to the nearest orphanage. We followed Maggie's directions precisely, and it took us a little over an hour to make the trip. It had warmed up some since this morning, but I still felt the chill seep into my skin until I wanted nothing more than to sit in front of a roaring fire, covered with a blanket, eating a piping hot bowl of soup and drinking gallons of coffee.

I laughed out loud at the picture. Jack turned to me with a questioning look.

"I'm having caffeine fantasies at the moment. I hadn't realized how much I would miss coffee."

He laughed. "That's one thing I don't think you're going to find here. Maggie told me that coffee is only slightly behind chocolate and cigarettes for in-demand black market items."

I shook my head. "It surprises me that in a place where just getting enough to eat is a struggle that people would even care about nonessentials like coffee and cigarettes. Why aren't they trading on the black market for sugar or flour?"

Jack shook his head. "No idea. But perhaps, just for a few moments, long enough to enjoy that coffee or that bar of chocolate, the world feels normal again. And maybe to some people, that feeling is worth any price."

I didn't say anything, surprised by Jack's flash of insight. We continued to walk, and I saw the large grey building Maggie had described. It looked as much like a prison as it did an orphanage. Three stories high with tiny windows all the way around. The front of the building was imposing, almost threatening in its severity. I couldn't imagine children living here. There was no yard or grass or swing set. It was almost a surprise that there weren't bars on the windows.

"Cheery-looking place," I commented as we approached the door.

"It looks like it was built out of solid granite, so maybe that's why it's one of the few buildings on this street that isn't damaged."

I looked around and saw he was right. Every

other building on this street had at least some bombing damage. Some looked as though they were a whisper away from falling down entirely. But there weren't even any cracks spidering along the massive walls of the orphanage. It stood like a sentinel, the lone survivor of a storm of destruction.

We walked up the steps, knocked on the massive wooden door, and waited. It was several moments before we heard the door open.

An older woman, mid-fifties perhaps, in a colorless dark dress covered by a white apron, stepped out onto the stairs and said something in hard, sharp German.

I turned slightly toward Jack and listened as he fired back at the woman. I had no idea what they were saying, but it didn't sound friendly. Although to me German almost never sounded friendly.

I waited patiently, either to be let in or to have the door slammed in our faces. At this point, I wasn't sure which was more likely.

Just when I thought the door was going to slam, the woman stepped aside and gestured for us to enter. As I stepped in front of Jack I muttered, "What was that about?"

"It appears we should have made an appointment to see the matron before coming."

I looked at him. "Do they have a telephone?"

"No."

"Then how?"

"Let's just say that this is one cranky lady, and in her mind, the lack of a telephone should not have made any difference."

I shook my head and continued on into the building. I looked at my surroundings and saw that I was in a foyer with a set of stairs and several hallways all pointing in different directions. The building smelled a little stale and a little dirty. The areas I could see so far didn't look dirty, but the air smelled distinctly of unwashed laundry.

The grumpy woman led us down one of the hallways, stopped at the first door, and rapped on it. A voice called out from inside.

The woman turned the door handle, pushed it open, and stepped aside to let us both in. Behind the desk sat a woman, about forty. She looked proper and efficient in her starched uniform, but a softness in her face made her look approachable.

Jack spoke to her in rapid German, and I was surprised and relieved when she answered in smooth English.

"Welcome, Mr. and Mrs. Fortune." I didn't wince, but it was close. "Come in, shut the door, and we can discuss the reason for your interest in our orphanage." She smiled, and although there were deep lines under her eyes, the smile looked sincere.

I crossed to the door, pushed it shut, and then moved toward one of the two chairs that were next to her desk. I sat down next to Jack and watched as he pulled our little packet of papers out of his pocket. The documents that explained our official reason for being in Berlin.

"It says here that your organization has permission from both the American and the German governments to take eight orphans back to the United States for adoption there. Is that right?"

"Actually, it will only be seven. We have a specific child, a relative of one of the members of our organization, who is going to be coming back with us. So we only have seven orphans that we can bring back with us."

She smiled, and this time it even lifted her weary eyes. "That's wonderful news. Why don't I tell you a little bit about our orphanage?" We both nodded, so she continued. "We house between 189 and 201 children at a time, ranging in ages from birth to twelve years old. We are currently running at capacity. Some of our children are officially displaced persons. That means that they were released from concentration camps at the end of the war, but for some reason or other they had no homes to return to. This is most often because the rest of their families died in the camps.

"We also have German children whose parents died in the war, and lastly we have illegitimate children. Often with fathers who were American or Russian or British soldiers. There is an ugly stigma attached to bearing children from these fathers, and that's why a lot of them end up at our doors."

Jack and I sat in stunned silence. I tried to imagine two hundred children, in this building alone, either orphaned or abandoned, and it made me feel ill.

The matron, however, seemed to view this as just a recitation of facts, and she continued. "Unfortunately there is quite a bit of paperwork involved with adopting this many children, and going through the proper government channels, but if we get started right away, I'm sure we can get this process going."

Jack nodded. The matron looked at me. "If you'd like, I could have one of the staff show you around the orphanage while your husband and I deal with the forms."

I smiled. "I'd love that."

"Lovely." She rose from behind her desk and crossed to the door. "Give me a moment, please, and I'll bring back one of our English-speaking staff members to give you the tour."

A young woman named Birgit, maybe twenty, was my tour guide. She spoke English well, having learned when she was living in the American sector. The first place she took me were the rooms where the children slept. Row after row of narrow cots, all neatly made and lined up with military precision.

The next room she brought me to was the nursery. I heard it long before I arrived. The sound of plaintive wailing coming from a chorus of lungs. I took a deep breath, preparing myself before we walked into the room for what I was going to see.

I still wasn't ready. The room was large with maybe twenty-five white metal cribs lined up in rows. The cribs were scratched and rusted in places, the walls the color of dirty dishwater, and the smell of unclean laundry and diapers was nearly overwhelming. But nothing was nearly as awful as the sight of the babies themselves. From my spot at the doorway I could only see the ones who were sitting or standing at the crib rails. The child closest to me looked to be about a year old. The baby could stand, holding the rail, and he, I thought it was a he, turned toward us as soon as we came into the room. He started to cry, but his voice was hoarse, and I watched as big fat tears streamed down his chubby face. His soul-rending sobs brought tears to my eyes, making me move across to his crib and lean over to lift him out. There didn't appear to be anyone in the room to tend to him, or any of the other wailing children.

A hand on my arm stopped me before I could lift him out.

"We don't pick the babies up; it only makes them cry more. They are taken out of their cribs to be fed and changed twice a day."

I turned to her, stunned. "How can they stay in their cribs all the time?" I asked. The little boy held his arms out to me, begging me with his gaze to come back, to lift him out.

I longed to, but Birgit shook her head no, and I took a step back. "We don't have enough workers to hold the babies, and they all must learn to cope with the way things are."

I felt a tear drip down my cheek as the little boy fell back on his bottom, huddled into a ball on his side, and cried into the mattress.

"He is not used to the way things are here. His mother only brought him to us a few weeks ago. He cries all the time." Birgit said it with what sounded like a modicum of sympathy.

I looked around the room and saw all of the other babies, most crying or at least whimpering, but some lying apathetically on the mattresses. The listless ones were almost more frightening. As though they had already accepted their fate.

Birgit pulled at my sleeve. "Let us go; we are upsetting them even more." She pulled me out of the room, and I felt sick as the din of wailing increased in pitch as the children watched us leave.

The dining hall was easier. It was almost lunchtime, and Birgit and I went into the kitchen to see if there was anything we could do to help get the meal ready. The cook, a stout, aproned woman who could have been anywhere between sixty and seventy years old, didn't understand English. Birgit spoke to her in German, and the older woman waved her spoon at us and snapped something before turning back to the huge pot in front of her.

"Hilda says we can get the water pitchers filled if we insist on invading her kitchen." Birgit said this with a smile, and I couldn't help but smile back.

"Is she always this friendly?" I asked.

"No, sometimes she's in a bad mood," Birgit said seriously.

We worked together getting pitchers of water filled and put out on the long tables. In a few minutes there was the sound of pounding feet and hushed childish voices.

Within minutes the dining hall doors flooded open and the children came pouring in. It was odd that there was a lot of noise from the crush of children but not one voice to be heard. No one spoke as they formed a line in front of the kitchen where Hilda was preparing to serve the soup she'd been stirring when we walked in.

"Why are they all so quiet?" I asked.

"Any child that speaks during the meal will be sent out of the dining hall without getting to eat," she whispered to me. "There is to be absolute silence at all times during meals."

I had a hard time believing that 150 or so children could be completely silent for an entire meal, but they proved me wrong. In a place like this, it was probably a major loss to miss a meal, even the slightly revolting looking, cloudy soup with dumplings that Hilda had served.

Within twenty minutes the children were finished, and Birgit had dismissed them all. When they had all trickled out of the large room, Birgit picked up two bowls and handed one to me. "We will have lunch now."

It wasn't a question, and I wondered if there was some way I could get out of it, but quickly decided that there wasn't a polite way. Besides, I'd barely been eating for the past two days, so I really shouldn't be picky about what I was served.

Hilda filled our bowls with a snort, and I tried not to look too closely at what was floating in the broth.

We sat down and ate our lunch in silence. The soup was mostly onion with a little bit of cabbage and a few potatoes. It wasn't as bad as it looked, although I realized after the first one that the dumplings were best swallowed whole with no chewing.

Birgit and I gave Hilda a hand at washing the dishes that were stacked all along the counters. I washed and soon discovered that there was little soap and less hot water. I did the best I could to get the dishes clean, and Birgit dried them all and put them away. Hilda gave us a grunt of thanks, or at least I assumed it was of thanks, as we left. Birgit took me back to the matron's office after that and knocked on the door. We were told to come in, and Birgit opened the door for me and ushered me inside.

Jack and the matron were hunched over papers, empty soup bowls on the desk next to them.

Birgit nodded and then slipped out of the room and shut the door behind her.

"So how's it going in here?"

Chapter 30

MAGGIE

NEVER HAD A DAY crawled by so slowly. Being trapped inside while others were working to effect her rescue didn't sit comfortably. Maggie lay down next to a napping Greta and let her weary eyes close.

ALGERIA 1941

At the outset of their first shift she and Lizzie were both assigned to surgical teams, picked because they both had training and experience in the operating room. There were four surgical teams, and on bad days, days with lots of casualties, the surgical teams could be operating every minute of their twelve-hour shifts, at least according to the stories one of the other surgical nurses told. Shirley was from Texas originally and was assigned to get the newcomers outfitted and to show them the ropes on their first night.

"We mostly see victims of shrapnel wounds, explosions, and of course the ever-popular gunshot wounds. This isn't like some Stateside hospital with fancy recovery wards and spotless operating theaters." She sounded wistful. "We usually have two patients going at one time, and it's stitch and switch. One moves out, another moves in."

Sounds horrifying, Maggie thought.

Her face must have betrayed what she was thinking, because Shirley laughed. "You'll get used to it soon enough."

And Shirley was right. It took a few days for Maggie to get used to the frantic pace, moving from one patient to the next, letting someone else deal with all of the follow-up care, but she did get used to it. In some ways it felt good, using her skills to help save lives. It was a new and strange feeling to have people depending on her, strange but good.

For better or for worse, today was a straight operating day. Her team's operating "theater" was being cleaned out to get ready for the shift change and the new patient. As she gowned up and scrubbed in, she saw two of the doctors come in behind her. Dr. Cullum McRae was first. His head was turned, talking to the man behind him. She couldn't make out the words, but the soft-spoken Scottish doctor laughed and then turned back in her direction. He caught her eye as she turned away from the sink, and he smiled. Following him was another surgeon on the night shift, Dr. Thomas Grant. Maggie felt a little sorry for Lizzie, who was assigned to Dr. Grant's team, as he was a demanding perfectionist and spent a lot of time yelling at the people around him. Dr. McRae, on the other hand, was as exacting as his colleague but was soft-spoken and fair to the people he worked with. Maggie felt lucky to work with such a skilled surgeon and kind man.

She moved into the sterile field and took her place beside the operating table. One of the things she liked about Dr. McRae was that he was interested in everyone on his team. He liked to know the people he worked with, where they came from, what their lives had been like before, all of the details that make up a person.

He pushed against the scrub room door with his back, his hands raised up in front of him to avoid touching anything. She watched as he and the rest of the members of their team took their places around the table. The anesthesiologist adjusted a few knobs, making sure that the patient was perfectly anesthetized, while everyone else got ready to work.

Everyone was silent for a while as the team worked. The clatter of metal hitting the sterile instrument tray was the only sound other than the occasional quiet order from Dr. McRae. Once the delicate part of the operation was over and the rest was cleaning, stitching, and dressing, he looked up. His eyes searched around the table before stopping at her.

"It's your turn today, Nurse O'Shayne."

"My turn?" Her face reddened. While she'd

enjoyed the question and answer period when it had involved the others, she wasn't at all keen on being the center of attention while he turned his relentless questions on her.

"Yes, you, Maggie."

It was the first time he'd called her by her first name, and it felt a little strange.

"You can start with where you're from and a little about your family."

She groaned inwardly, but she wasn't going to make an issue of it by not answering. "I'm from New York City. I was born and raised there, lived in the same Brooklyn neighborhood my entire life."

"And your family?"

"My mother and father emigrated from Ireland soon after they got married. Both of them loved New York. I'm an only child, and my parents were both killed in an auto accident almost seven years ago." She hoped that the recitation of facts would satisfy him and that the questions would end now.

"And that would have made you an orphan at what, age fourteen?" he asked, not backing off as most people would at the mention of her parents' death.

"Fifteen."

"And your extended family took you in after that?" Maggie raised her eyes to his for a second, appalled that he would keep pushing this line of questioning. He met her gaze, and she saw no hesitance or guilt there. She saw interest and determination instead. For a second Maggie thought she saw something else too, but she looked back down quickly and tried to remember her place in the interrogation.

"I had no extended family in America; some neighbors, friends of my parents, took me in after that. Letting me live with them so that I could finish school without having to leave the neighborhood. I lived with them until I enlisted."

"And what made you decide to enlist?" he asked.

They all worked automatically, and for a second she imagined sticking him with the suture needle she was holding for him. That might teach him not to pry. Shaking the thought from her head, she concentrated once again on the patient.

"What made you decide to enlist?" he asked again.

"I wanted to help people." She left it at that, not caring anymore that her answers were abrupt enough to be considered rude at this point.

"And what about your life back home? Surely there was someone special that you had to leave behind. Is there a man in your life waiting for you to come back home? Did you leave someone brokenhearted by coming here?"

It felt like he'd taken his trusty scalpel and calmly cut open her deepest wound. Infected guilt and regret. For a second she seriously considered walking out of the theater, scrubbing out, and facing whatever disciplinary action would be meted out for her actions. But then she looked down at the soldier lying helpless on the table and forced herself to act like a professional.

"Some things are none of your business, Doctor. I think your patient would benefit from your complete attention, don't you?" The words were bitterly cold, and the head nurse's face flashed toward her, but Maggie continued working and refused to meet her gaze. It was inappropriate to be rude to one of the doctors, but Maggie was past caring.

The silence around the table was thunderous. She'd crossed a very big line, but so had he with his way too personal questions. She steeled her spine and raised her eyes to meet his. Choosing not to read whatever message his eyes were trying to send above his operating mask, she kept her gaze cold and detached.

Dr. McRae's eyes stayed on her as he continued to stitch. "You are correct, Nurse O'Shayne. My questions were out of line. I apologize."

She was surprised at his public contrition, but she didn't soften, just nodded and went back to work.

Eventually the tense mood around the table lifted, but she continued to work in silence, praying for the shift to finally end.

Dr. McRae came by the nurses' quarters a few hours after the shift ended. One of the other nurses came to get her since men were not allowed into the nurses' tent.

When she heard who was out there she wanted to refuse but knew that it was a bad idea. If he'd come to dress her down for her behavior in the OR, then she needed to face it like a grown-up.

164

She left the tent and saw him standing a few feet away from the door, his back to her. She watched him for a second or two before announcing her presence. He looked exhausted. Bone weary. And she realized that it was the first time she'd seen him look anything other than confident and in control.

"Mary-Katherine said that you wanted to speak to me," she said, slamming the door on the sudden surge of compassion she felt for him.

She watched, fascinated, as the look of weariness faded and the competence slid back into place. "Yes, Nurse O'Shayne. I need to speak with you."

She straightened her shoulders and prepared herself for whatever lecture was coming.

"I need to ask your forgiveness for my behavior earlier today." The soft Scottish burr made the words seem soft as an embrace. She looked at him, stunned by the words. "I was out of line and prying, and I'm very sorry. I could see that you were uncomfortable, but my curiosity overrode propriety. I am sorry that I embarrassed you in front of our colleagues."

She had no idea what to say.

He cleared his throat, and she saw for the first time how uncomfortable he looked.

Even though part of her wanted to stay hard, the better half of her took pity on him. "I accept your apology, Dr. McRae. And I suppose I should apologize for my rudeness as well." The last part came out grudgingly.

His face relaxed and folded into a smile at her reluctant apology. "First, please call me Cullum when we're not on duty, and second, you have no need to apologize. I must say though, that I have never been quite so thoroughly put in my place before." His eyes crinkled with humor, inviting her to laugh along with him.

She blew out a breath that held the last of her anger and then laughed too.

For a few days after their argument and his apology, working with Cullum was awkward, but he smiled whenever he saw her and eventually the awkwardness faded. In fact, when they finished their shift, they occasionally sat together in the mess hall to eat. He'd never again crossed the boundaries she'd set out around her private life, instead telling her about his childhood in rural Scotland.

He told her about growing up outside of Aberdeen, going to medical school and then eventually emigrating to America. He'd settled down in Kentucky someplace, and had worked for several years as the only surgeon in a Kentucky mining town.

The more he spoke, the more she found she liked him. He missed his family in Scotland but also longed to see more of the world than just the silver stones of Aberdeen.

After a while she almost wanted to tell him more about her life, about Jack, but there was still an invisible wall between them, one of her own making, and she wasn't sure if she was ready to breach it.

Maggie woke with the events in her dream as clear in her mind as they'd been the day they'd happened. Blowing out a breath she forced her mind back to the present.

Chapter 31

ALLIE

JACK AND I WALKED back toward Maggie's place and I told him about what I'd seen at the orphanage. He told me that the matron, whose name was Vivienne, would be selecting the children who would come with us. I agreed that it would be easier than trying to select just a handful of children out of so many.

The trek back seemed much longer than it had this morning, and darkness was beginning to fall as we got closer.

"Have you got a plan for what you're going to be doing when you go out with Maggie tonight?" I asked as we walked.

"Maggie's going to take me to the American sector and we're going to scout around and see if we can find out any more about the troop movement rumor. If it's true I'll talk to whoever is in charge and try to find space on a truck, with enough room for all of the children, then we would have a definite time and way to get out of Berlin."

"And what about Maggie? How would she get on? Of all the people who are looking for her, an entire convoy of American soldiers is not going to miss the fact that a non-passported American woman with red hair was trying to leave the country."

"Obviously we're not talking about them knowing she's on board. Now, ask me how we're going to do that, and I can tell you I have no idea, but we'll take this one step at a time. For now, we need to secure transportation. After that, we'll see."

I nodded. It made sense to me. At the most, the vehicle we'd brought into Berlin could only hold six people, and we needed something with room for at least eleven. I wasn't sure how we were going to get the car back, we'd never discussed it, but surely either Jack or I could drive behind the convoy.

"What do you think it says on those documents of Maggie's?" I asked, in a voice barely above a whisper. I shoved my hands deep inside the pockets of my woolen coat, wiggling my fingers to try to warm them up.

"I don't know, but I think she's going to have to tell us, whether she wants to or not. I have the feeling that we're not going to really understand the scope of the situation until we understand exactly what Maggie has stumbled onto."

I nodded. I'd been thinking the same thing. I

could see why Maggie was so reluctant to tell us, but working blind wasn't a great option.

Jack moved ahead of me, leading the way around the back of Maggie's building after checking to make sure no one was around or watching. He uncovered the stairwell entrance and gestured for me to enter before him. I went right to the bottom and watched as he entered and then took care to cover the entrance properly again.

I knocked softly on the door and within seconds Maggie pulled it open. She had a look of relief on her face that she quickly disguised with a neutral expression. Before she shuttered herself off, I'd seen something in her eyes that gave me pause. It was a look of naked joy to see Jack again. As though she'd missed him desperately in the hours he'd been away.

I wondered if Jack had seen it. I hoped he had, that it would prompt him to do something. They were so cagey with each other I felt like kicking both of them. Neither one was willing to step forward and say, "I missed you and I still love you," when both their eyes and their actions screamed out the truth.

After Maggie smothered the emotions burning in her eyes, I nearly sighed as I walked past her. I wanted to shake her, shake Jack. What I wouldn't give to have the chance they'd been given. What I wouldn't have done to get to see David again, to have the chance to tell him that I loved him, had loved him for years. A sting burnt at my eyes, and I blinked once, hard enough to clear them and push back any more moisture that wanted to rise.

Jack followed me inside, and I heard Maggie shut the door behind us.

"How did it go? Are you sure no one saw you come in here?" she asked.

"I made sure." Jack moved over to the corner where Greta stood and said something to her, too quiet for me to overhear, then turned back to Maggie.

"We can go out in an hour or so. Let's wait until it's fully dark."

Chapter 32

MAGGIE

MAGGIE SHRUGGED on her much-worn woolen coat and buttoned it as high as it went. She knew exactly how cold it could get overnight this time of year. They had a several-mile walk ahead of them, and she couldn't help but wonder how it was going to feel to spend the next few hours alone with Jack. So far Allie had been a buffer between them, and it had been both a blessing and a source of frustration. Maggie didn't know if she was ready to face Jack on her own yet. He was, in ways, the same person she'd known, but in other, integral ways, a total stranger.

170

She led the way out of the apartment and out into the darkened streets in silence. The plan was to go and find a friend, someone Maggie knew she could trust, and see if they could find out what was happening. Marion was a coworker and a friend, had been for years. Maggie had asked her to keep an eye on the situation in the American sector for her. This wouldn't be the first time Marion would be woken in the middle of the night by her old friend.

Jack walked in silence beside her. His hands stuffed in his pockets, his shoulders hunched against the cold wind, and his hat pulled down low, his expression was impossible to read. As they walked, Maggie's mind drifted back to countless times they'd walked side by side in silence. Her hand in his, feeling, for that moment, that as long as he was beside her, she was safe and protected. It seemed so right after everything, him walking beside her once again.

She shook the thought away, forcing her concentration back to the task at hand: getting the information they needed to get them all out of the city safely.

The quick conversation at Marion's had produced little but the fact that she'd heard the rumors of a big American troop movement as well. Her rumors had a date attached. Two nights from tonight. Marion gave her a quick hug while Jack watched from the apartment corridor. "Be careful," she whispered. "Write to me, let me know you're safe once you get out."

Maggie nodded, tears stinging her eyes. "I promise."

With that Maggie turned and headed out of the apartment building, Jack following along behind her. She took a deep breath, trying to ease the swell of emotion. It had been so hard to turn away from Marion, knowing that she'd probably never see her again. She waited for Jack to catch up with her just outside the apartment building. The street was deserted, but they still needed to get off the main road.

As soon as he was within a few feet she set off in a new direction. Jack had asked her to show him where the American base was so that he could go back later. She wasn't going to take him all the way there, it was too dangerous, but she'd take him close enough that she could give him simple directions from there.

It was only a half-mile walk and they made it in complete silence. Finally she'd come as close as she was going to go. Just the thought of getting any closer made her breath thicken in her chest.

Stepping behind the corner of a building she pointed slightly east. "It's over there. About a quarter mile. You'll find it if you go straight that direction. You'll end up along a fence. From there you just follow the fence east until you get to the main gate. The base acts as sort of an American embassy for Berlin. If you've got an American passport, it will at least get you on the base to talk to someone there."

Jack nodded and adjusted the crown of his hat. "You stay here. I'm going to go and check things out. I want to get the lay of the land," he said, avoiding her eyes.

The thought of staying here alone, waiting for him, made her stomach jump, but she nodded anyway.

"I'll be right back," he said, then took off into the darkness.

She watched his movements for as long as she could, her gaze trailing him, until he finally blurred into the shadows around him.

Maggie sighed, feeling fear and unease seep into her bones. She'd been so careful, for so long, not to stand still, not to be vulnerable, not to put herself at risk, and yet here she was, alone in the dark, waiting for Jack to come back.

It was more than an hour before Jack returned, and her nerves were stretched to the breaking point. When he reappeared beside her, it took everything in her power not to jump and scream at the suddenness of his arrival. She covered her pounding heart with her hand and closed her eyes.

"We should head back now. It will be daylight in a few hours."

They walked in silence for several minutes.

"How did it go?" Maggie asked when it appeared he wasn't going to say anything.

He blew out a frustrated breath and shoved his hat back an inch. "It could have gone better. I saw the poster of you. It's not a bad likeness really."

"Ah." She understood his silence now. She hesitated for a moment, needing her words to come out just right. "Jack, if the time comes and I can't get out of Berlin, or if anything happens to me, I need you to promise that you'll get Greta out and keep her safe. No matter what it takes."

He grunted.

"I'm serious. I need you to promise me."

"Promise that I'll leave you behind to die? I'm making no such promise, Maggie. I'm not leaving your side, for any reason. Allie can take care of Greta and get her out, but no way on earth am I promising you anything other than I am going to get you out."

She squeezed her eyes shut in frustration. "Jack, you have to promise. You're the only person in the world I would trust with her. Please."

"Don't ask me that!" He shouted the words and the sound echoed up and down the empty street. "I can't make that promise. I won't leave you behind, so stop asking." His voice was much quieter this time, but the steel core of determination in the words warned her that there would be no changing his mind tonight.

The rest of the walk home passed in tense silence.

Chapter 33

ALLIE

I WAS BROUGHT awake by the sound of the door creaking open. I rubbed my eyes and pushed myself up from the mattress. I sat up in time to see Maggie come into the apartment, followed by Jack. Over his shoulder I saw that the sky was an iron grey color that told me I'd slept all night. The sun would be up within the hour. I felt better, refreshed and a little shocked at the realization that I must have slept for eight hours straight. Beside me, Greta was still asleep, and I moved as slowly as possible to avoid disturbing her. Once on my feet I stretched discreetly and tried to get my brain working.

"How did it go?" I asked.

Maggie and Jack exchanged a look that I couldn't interpret. "It was a long night, but we found out that the convoy is leaving tomorrow night. Christmas night."

"That soon?" I asked. "Can we be ready to go by then?"

"We're going to have to be," Maggie said. "This actually might be our only chance for anyone to get in or out for quite a while." I looked to Maggie, waiting for her to explain her statement.

"There's talk of a Soviet blockade of all routes

175

out of the city. Because Berlin itself is in the Soviet side of Germany, if they close up the borders, no one and nothing is going to get in or out of the city."

"Do you think there's much truth to the rumors?" I asked, feeling a little skeptical.

"Let's just put it this way, the American military is taking it seriously. That's what all of the troop movement is about. They think the doors are basically going to close to supplies and people any day."

I felt a little curl of unease. She was right. Whether we were ready or not, we needed to get out of this country.

"Did you find out anything else? Will we be able to find a way onto the convoy?"

Jack shrugged. "I don't think it should be a problem. If we show them our American passports and adoption paperwork, I don't think they'll be hard to convince to offer us safe passage out of Berlin. I'm going to go see if I can make official arrangements later today."

"What about Maggie?" I said, looking at her, including her in the question. "She's extremely recognizable. Any ideas yet on how we're going to get her out?"

Jack's eyes narrowed. "Not yet, but I'm still working on it."

I nodded. It was a start. The bones of a plan were in place, but it was still all a little flimsy for me.

"How'd you sleep?" Maggie asked once Jack had gone into the other room to get cleaned up for the day.

"Great actually," I said. "Greta was making noise, like she was having a nightmare, and so I went over to sit with her. I must have fallen asleep, because the next thing I knew, you and Jack were back and it was morning."

Maggie smiled at me. "You look more rested."

"I am. I feel pretty good actually." I took a deep breath, trying to decide if I should ask or not. "Can I ask something personal?"

Maggie hesitated. "Okay."

"Did something happen between you and Jack last night? You both seemed . . ." I trailed off, looking for the right word, ". . . a little awkward when you got back."

Maggie grabbed the broom from the corner where it rested and began sweeping a floor that didn't need swept. She was silent long enough that I'd decided she wasn't going to answer, so I was surprised when she spoke.

"We fought about something. It's hard getting through to that man sometimes. He can be very stubborn. I think he's regretting ever having come here."

I leaned against the wall and thought for a moment. "Could I give you a piece of advice?" I asked.

She sighed. "Sure."

I looked toward Jack's door to make sure it was still firmly closed before speaking. "You both have been given this second chance, and you both are letting things, said and unsaid, stand between you." I paused, checking on the door again, but it remained firmly shut. "I would give anything to be in your position. To have a second chance with the person I love. Don't waste this opportunity."

"You lost someone?" Maggie asked.

I nodded, but didn't elaborate. "Right now we're talking about you. You and Jack. My advice to you is not to let your pride stand in the way of letting him know how you really feel." I paused. "Because you do love him, don't you?"

Maggie looked me straight in the eyes and nodded almost imperceptibly.

I didn't let my smile show. It was as much of an admission as I was likely to get from her, but it confirmed what I already knew.

"One day you're going to have to tell me your story," she said. "It would seem only fair."

I laughed, but there was no humor sliding through it. "My story does not come with a happily ever after, and I'm starting to think it might just be better left in the past. Because carrying a torch for someone you haven't seen or heard from in eight years is probably not the best way to live."

"It's funny how life goes on, but in some ways it really doesn't."

I nodded, surprised that she understood. I'd made a life for myself in the years since David left, I had a career and friends, but when it came to love, I'd stood absolutely still. Life had gone on, but she was right—in a lot of ways it really hadn't.

Chapter 34

JACK LEFT WITHIN an hour or so of bringing Maggie back. He headed back for the American sector to see if he could arrange for safe passage out of Berlin for eight orphans and two Americans. We'd have to find a way to sneak Maggie across once we had all of the arrangements in place.

He looked weary as he was leaving, and I had the urge to hug him, but more, I wished Maggie would walk up to him and wrap her arms around him. More than anything right now, I think he needed to know how she really felt about him. I could only imagine how the fear of not having his feelings for Maggie returned was wearing him down.

I planned on spending the morning working on my mother's request. Having no idea where to start looking for my mother's mysterious priest wasn't a good enough excuse not to go looking. Not knowing how short our time in Berlin might be, I needed to get started tracking the man down as soon as possible. My mother said he'd been a priest at St. Martin's church, but when I'd asked Maggie about it, there'd been no light of recognition in her eyes. So either it was in a part of the city she wasn't familiar with or the church hadn't survived the war.

Armed with nothing more than my warm woolen coat, a pocketful of chocolate, and a few German phrases written on a slip of paper courtesy of Maggie, I headed out. Asking around seemed like the smart thing to do, but I kept my head down and avoided eye contact until I was at least a dozen blocks from Maggie's home. I didn't want to call attention to myself until I was too far away to be traced back to Maggie's derelict hiding spot.

The air was cold and heavy, and clouds hung low over the city like a smoldering blanket. I shoved my free hand into my pocket, huddled deep into the felted wool protection of my coat, and held the box close to my chest. I lifted my face to the wind for a second and sniffed. It smelled like snow, sharper and less sweet than the smell of impending rain. The distinctive smell of a coming snowstorm brought my mind to full whirring life. My time for searching was going to be shorter than I'd thought. I looked around, realizing for the first time there were fewer people on the streets today than I was used to, and the ones who were out were moving fast, eyes straight ahead. Apparently they'd realized before I had that we were probably in for bad weather. It also occurred to me for the first time since arriving that today was Christmas Eve. Wandering the streets of

Berlin was a far cry from attending the annual Christmas Eve party my parents hosted. I felt a pang of homesickness at the thought of missing it.

I picked up my pace and looked around for someone to question. It made sense to look for an older person, someone who would know the city well and would remember what it had been like before the war. I surveyed the street and tried to imagine what it had all looked like then.

It was like trying to imagine the shape of a block tower that had been knocked over by a careless child. My mind flashed back to a dimly remembered Bible reference to not one stone being left on top of another. That's what this looked like. The destruction on this street looked as though no stone had been left on top of another.

Perhaps because of the destruction, there were few people on this street. I turned at the next corner, wandering, mostly aimlessly. I stroked the surface of the box with gloved fingers, feeling the wood's smoothness even through the wool.

I tried to imagine what deep dark secret from my mother's past this box could represent. She hadn't given any details, and that lack alone was enough to send my mind off weaving tales of what it meant.

I turned another corner, looked up, and blinked. I hadn't seen a soul for the last several minutes, but suddenly there were hundreds of people crowded on the street in front of me. I kept walking and saw that most of them were older women. I looked to see what everyone was standing around for. Above the mostly kerchiefed heads of the crowd was a small building. Apparently the people standing outside were attempting to get inside. Most of the people held a card, and that's when I realized what this was. This was a ration line. The building must be a store, and they must have something, food or supplies, that people were lining up to buy. Judging from the number of people and the size of the store I doubted that everyone was going to leave satisfied today. Not great for the people standing out in the cold, but the crowd was perfect for my purposes.

I slipped the scrap of paper out of my pocket and held it up. Maggie had written three phrases down for me, and I practiced them in my head, hoping that I wasn't going to butcher the pronunciation so badly that the words would be unrecognizable.

I found a likely candidate and made my way over to her. "Do you know where St. Martin's church is?" I asked in halting, pathetic German. The woman looked at me, the lines in her face folding into deep crevasses of bafflement. I held back a sigh and tried again. More slowly this time. With actions.

The old woman shook her head, made a sound of disgust, and turned away. Strike one. I took another look at my paper, mouthed the words to myself once again, and found another candidate.

The second interaction had the same result as the first. Apparently I was utterly incomprehensible. I looked around, feeling frustration seethe within me at this block. Maybe I should have asked Jack, of the fluent German, to come with me, but for some reason I hadn't wanted him involved in my mother's quest. Shaking my head I forced myself to be honest, at least with myself —I hadn't wanted him to be a part of this crazy case because he'd already seen too much of my family struggles. Some things were best kept private. With no idea what I was getting into on my mother's behalf, I had an instinctive desire to keep this investigation to myself. Which meant an utter lack of ability to communicate.

I sighed. The line in front of me didn't seem to be moving much. I wondered if I should give communication one more try when a shrill whistle pierced the air. Every head turned in the direction of the sound, including mine. There stood two uniformed soldiers, and I heard a collective groan from the crowd around me. One of the soldiers cupped his hands around his mouth to project his voice, and snapped out a dozen words in German. Another collective sigh and then almost as one, the people around me turned and dispersed in all directions. Within a minute I was standing in front of the shop, with only the soldiers remaining. With no idea what had made everyone rush off, I wondered for a second if one of the buildings near here was in danger of collapse, or if the soldiers had relayed some other important message that I hadn't understood. I turned to leave but stopped at the sound of a shouted command from behind me. My hands tightened on the box, but I forced myself to relax before I turned back to face the two men.

Before I had the chance to turn all the way around another command was issued. I had no idea what they were saying, but the tone was unmistakable. They were telling me to do something and they were losing patience that I wasn't complying. I hurried to face them. "I'm sorry, I don't speak German," I said in my most compliant voice.

The two men moved closer, crossing the square until they were less than three feet in front of me. As they approached I recognized the French military uniform, and breathing a sigh of relief I switched from English to French.

"I'm sorry, I didn't understand what you said to the crowd before." I spoke in French, keeping my voice soft and submissive. I wanted both of these men holding guns to catalogue me as a non-threat.

"We told the people that the supplies had run out. There is no more. The store is empty." The man spoke so rapidly I had trouble catching all of the words. I looked, but saw no softening in either man's face or posture. I considered asking them about St. Martin's church, but a little voice in my head told me not to mention my destination.

"I shall go then too," I said, deciding that retreat

seemed like the best option at the minute. I wasn't sure why I felt so nervous in the presence of these men, but I didn't have a good feeling, and I wanted to get away as quickly as possible. Once again my hand tightened on the box, and I pulled it closer to my chest.

"What is that? What are you carrying?" The words came out jagged and hard. The soldier stretched out his gun and pointed its muzzle at my chest, or more correctly, at the box.

The hair on the back of my neck stood up and I thought quickly. "It's just a box. A Christmas gift I'm delivering." I felt a flush of unease at the sharpening gaze of both soldiers. The last thing I wanted was to pique their interest in me. I was supposed to be traveling covertly for Maggie's sake, and here I was drawing attention to myself, drawing the attention of soldiers no less.

The soldier with the gun pointed at me took another step closer until the end of the rifle barrel was only inches from me. He held out his other hand. "Hand over the box," he ordered.

A trickle of perspiration slid down the side of my neck. I kept my eyes on his, not daring to look away. I pulled the box out of my coat and placed it slowly into his outstretched hand.

I said a quick prayer for safety as I watched the soldier turn the beautiful wooden rectangle over in his hands. He hefted it as though surprised by its lack of weight. I winced as he shook it violently. His expression turned to frustration, and he turned back to me. "What is this? What's inside?"

I took a deep breath before speaking. "It's Japanese wooden art," I explained. "There's nothing inside." He glared at me, disbelief apparent on his face. I watched in horror as he placed the box on the ground and raised the butt of his gun as though he was going to smash it down on top of the box.

Without thinking I took a step forward and grabbed the man's arm and shoved it out of alignment with the box. Off balance his gun came down and bounced off of pavement instead of my mother's box. It took me a second to realize how foolish my actions were. It was only a box, and here I was at the mercy of two armed soldiers, in a country where I had no business being, trying to extricate a woman who called herself the most wanted person in all of Germany. What was I doing risking everything over some silly box my mother had asked me to deliver? I saw the expression on both soldiers' faces change to fury at my actions.

In seconds there were two guns pointed directly at my chest. As far as I could tell I had two courses of action in front of me. I could apologize, take a step back, and let my mother's box and her mystery be ground to splinters, or I could fight. The odds didn't look good, what with them armed with guns and me armed with nothing more than chocolate bars in my pockets, but I knew without having to think about it that I wasn't going to let either of these men keep me from fulfilling my promise to my mother.

"You can't break that. It doesn't even belong to me," I said, taking the offensive and praying that neither of these men was really in a shooting mood today.

Both men seemed taken aback at my lack of cowering. "We can do whatever we like."

I shook my head. "You have no reason to do this. I am just delivering this gift." I calculated in my head the chance that these two men would react in the manner I expected. It wasn't a good chance, but it was a chance, and I was willing to take the risk.

"To whom?" The soldier on the left sneered the question at me.

"Father Heinrich Neumann." I emphasized the word *Father,* hoping it would have the effect I was looking for.

"Father? A priest?" I wasn't sure, but I thought I saw one of the men pale, and I nearly smiled at the quick sign of the cross that the other one made, almost unconsciously. I'd guessed right. Neither man would be as keen to destroy the property of a priest. A nameless woman, sure, but not a symbol of church authority they'd been raised to respect and fear, not likely.

One of the men took a tiny step back, and I knew

that if I was careful I could get out of this situation almost unscathed. I tried a small smile. "I understand your suspicions, and I am impressed by your commitment to duty, but I assure you that I am simply on an errand to present this gift to the Father. I am very sorry for disturbing your patrol. Please, if you would just let me go I will take this to Father Neumann immediately and then get out of the storm." While we'd been standing there, the snow had begun to fall in huge wet flakes. Already there was a dusting on the concrete around us.

They looked at each other. One nodded, and the other turned back to me. "Be on your way then. And stay out of trouble from here on out."

I dropped my chin, nodded, and bent down to pick up the box. I felt relief well up inside me when I held it safely in my arms again.

Immediately I turned and headed out of the square. The snow was falling heavily now, and I was going to have to postpone the search for Father Neumann until later. As I walked the circuitous route back to Maggie's house I wondered what had come over me. I'd put everything at risk for that silly box. Not quite understanding why unraveling my mother's mystery had become so important to me, I just pulled the box tighter into my chest and picked up my pace. Answers would have to wait.

Chapter 35

MAGGIE

ALLIE HAD COME back from her mysterious errand covered in snow and freezing cold. Maggie and Allie had worked side by side in silence to prepare the evening meal. Maggie tried to force her thoughts away from the worrying reality that supplies were running out. Other than chocolate, they had two days' worth of food at the outside. Once they had the stew put together and set over the stove fire to heat, Allie excused herself to go and change. Maggie continued stirring.

ALGERIA 1941

They'd been in Africa about six months before she noticed that Lizzie was acting strangely. The other nurse was forgetful, distracted, and at times almost giddy. One night before their shift Maggie caught her giggling to herself in the mirror.

"That's it. Enough is enough. You need to tell me what's going on with you. You are either going insane, or you have a secret."

She whirled away from the mirror, grinning, and laughed again. "I've got the best secret."

Maggie's eyebrows flew up. "Spit it out, Lizzie."

Lizzie's grin got bigger, and she dragged Maggie

to her bed and sat her down on the edge of it. "What are you doing on Saturday?" she asked.

Maggie stared at her, wondering if she could possibly be serious. "The same thing I do every day. Working."

"Is there any chance you could forgo sleep for one day to make it to a very special event?"

Her curiosity was officially piqued, and her patience with her roommate's secrecy was reaching an end. She crossed her arms over her chest. "What is going on, Lizzie?"

"Well, on Saturday morning I'm going to be traveling across to Morocco, and I want you to come with me."

"Why would we drive five hours just for that? What's in Morocco?"

"I'm getting married there, so I thought it would be worth the trip." She laughed at Maggie's dumbfounded expression, then continued. "And I was sorta hoping that you'd want to come along and be my maid of honor."

Maggie needed several seconds to form a coherent thought. "And who, may I ask, is the groom?"

Lizzie laughed again and her whole face lit up. "Gerald Black."

"Dr. Black? From the day shift?"

She grinned. "We started talking when I wasn't sleeping and it sort of snowballed from there," she explained with a smile.

"And you waited until now to tell me because . . ."

"'Cause I wasn't sure he felt the same about me as I did about him. Since he asked me to marry him this morning, I would assume that means he feels the same."

It took a few moments for Maggie's brain to process the information, but after a few seconds she felt a grin stretch across her face. "Congratulations then." It needed a second to sink in.

Maggie stood up and wrapped her arms around her friend for a big hug.

"One more thing," she said after Maggie had finally let go. "I'd like you to come up to Morocco with us, but would you mind getting a ride back with Gerald's best man? We have two days of leave for our honeymoon, so we won't be going back straightaway."

"Of course. Who's his best man?" she asked, not really caring.

"Cullum McRae." There was an unreadable look in Lizzie's eyes as she told Maggie.

"Sure, that's fine," Maggie said. A little flicker of nervousness flared in her belly, but she squelched it, focusing instead on her happiness for Lizzie.

They got permission to leave for the day on Saturday as long as the wedding party was back in time for their evening shift. They all set out early as the driving would take most of the day. It felt strange for Maggie to be in nice clothes instead of military garb. From the look on Cullum's face the sight of her in her one good suit was a surprise. He looked handsome and a bit like a stranger in his suit too.

Feeling slightly awkward, Maggie was glad she was driving up with Lizzie and that Gerald and Cullum would be in the other vehicle. She resolved to concentrate on her time with Lizzie and not to think ahead to the five-hour drive back to the hospital when it would be just her and Cullum.

She and Lizzie laughed and reminisced the entire way up. She seemed remarkably calm for someone getting married in a few hours. Maggie knew she would have been a basket case, but Lizzie was positively glowing.

Once they'd been on the road for a few hours conversation settled, and Maggie spent her time watching the African countryside slide by. They stayed along the coast, and she marveled at the stark beauty of the landscape.

When they finally arrived in Casablanca, her stomach was twisted up with the nerves Lizzie didn't seem to be feeling.

There was a large military contingent in Morocco, and Lizzie and Gerald had made the trek because there were several chaplains in the city who could perform the wedding. Lieutenant Colonel Beeman had made all of the arrangements, so they just followed the directions he'd provided and they ended up outside a beautiful stone ruin. It might have been a church or a mosque at one point, but the open air arches showed a spectacular view out toward the sea. The chaplain was waiting for them. In the open air, with the sea on one side and the white city on the other, Gerald and Lizzie exchanged their vows.

The simplicity of the ceremony and the setting was so beautiful Maggie felt her eyes fill. It struck her how much she'd changed since the last wedding she'd attended. Thoughts of Jack made her sad and a little lonely, but she brushed the feelings off and brought her attention back to the couple in front of her.

Wiping a tear away Maggie watched the sea crash behind the couple and prayed that God would bless their marriage.

They weren't able to linger long. Maggie hugged Lizzie, kissed her on the cheek, and congratulated Gerald. Cullum congratulated them too, complimenting his friend on marrying such a lovely woman, and then they took their leave. She doubted Gerald or Lizzie even noticed when they were gone. They just continued to beam at each other.

Cullum led her back to the Jeep, and she got in, still sighing over the loveliness of the ceremony. He looked dashing in his dark suit, his black hair with its streaks of silver tidy for once. Maggie watched him out of the corner of her eye as he got into the driver's seat. He hesitated before starting the vehicle, as though he wanted to say something, but apparently thought better of it and just cranked the engine instead.

They drove in silence for a while, but as they were

about to leave the city, Maggie spoke up. "Do we have a little time to explore a market? I'd love to stop and get a little fresh fruit before heading back."

"Sure. I think we've got just enough time for that." He swung the Jeep over and parked next to the small open-air bazaar they'd been about to pass.

He threw his door open, got out, and rounded to her side to open her door before she even had a chance to reach for the handle.

A little hesitant, Maggie let him help her out of the Jeep, placing her hand in his.

They wandered the stalls of the market, enjoying the sunny day and the exotic merchandise.

They found a fruit stall and bought a few pieces, enough to share when they got back. Most of the fruits were things she'd never tried before, but the smells enticed her. One smelled especially delicious, and she reserved it for the drive home.

When they had the fruit, they headed back to the Jeep, but she was distracted by a table full of lace. She moved closer to see beautiful lengths of hand-tatted lace. Maggie picked up a length of it. "Oh, I wish we'd had a chance to pick this up for Lizzie before the wedding. A wedding veil would have been nice." She draped the lace over her hair and turned to him. "It would have been beautiful, don't you think?"

He was closer than she'd realized, two feet away at most, and he looked down at her. Her breath caught in her throat. "Very beautiful," he said, his voice soft.

She stood, frozen, and watched as he took a step toward her, resting his hands on her shoulders, leaning down to kiss her gently. Maggie's breath backed up in her lungs as panic swept over her.

She took a huge step back.

He just looked at her, his eyes unreadable. He gently took the forgotten length of lace from her hands and laid it back onto the table. Without a word he reached out his hand for hers and led the way back to the Jeep.

They didn't speak for the first several minutes. Cullum just drove, and she stared out at the landscape flashing by, not really seeing it this time.

After about fifteen minutes of awkward silence Cullum finally spoke. He turned to meet her eyes again and said the one thing guaranteed to make her blood run cold. "I think I'm in love with you, Maggie."

"What are you doing?" Allie's voice broke into her thoughts as she reentered the room, changed and looking warmer.

"Thinking about the past," she answered honestly.

"Dangerous pastime," Allie said, her voice quiet, but knowing. "Regrets?" She sounded hesitant, as though she wished she hadn't asked, but couldn't help herself.

Maggie felt a small smile lift the corners of her lips. "A few. You?"

"Oh yeah."

Chapter 36

ALLIE

I didn't notice until Maggie lit the candles that there was something special about the apartment. Maggie had cleaned the place spotless, and in the corner there was a pile of evergreen branches, boughs that brought the smell of pine inside. The smell made me realize why she was making a special effort.

"It's Christmas Eve."

Maggie laughed softly. "Not much escapes you, does it, Detective?"

I laughed. "The place looks nice." The words trailed off unconvincingly.

Maggie looked around at the cracked walls and ramshackle bits of furniture, making her point without saying a word.

"How about it looks nicer?"

She smiled. "That's what I was aiming for. Nicer. If you have to spend Christmas here because of me, we should at least try and have a few hours to celebrate Christmas Eve together."

Suddenly glad that she'd thought of it, and glad that I wouldn't miss Christmas altogether, I took a step toward Maggie and gave her a quick hug. It surprised me every bit as much as it surprised her, I think.

The sound of Jack entering brought our attention to the door and kept me from having to explain my spontaneous display of emotion, which I'm not sure I could have anyway.

We saw Jack's back first. He pushed the door open with his shoulder, apparently carrying something, but hiding it from our view as he entered.

The sight of what he carried brought a grin to my face as he turned. In one hand he held a burlap sack and in the other he carried the biggest goose I'd ever seen in my life. Pink and knobbly-fleshed, it wasn't a Christmas miracle, yet I couldn't ignore the rush of emotion that made it feel like it was.

"Where . . . ?" Maggie trailed off, unable to verbalize her question past the astonishment visible on her face.

A grin split Jack's face at the openmouthed astonishment from all of us. "I traded most of our remaining chocolate for this goose, a few potatoes, and an onion. Think we can find a way to make this into a Christmas meal?"

The sheer delight on Greta's face made me laugh. It was so like Jack to pull off the impossible like this. After a second Maggie started to giggle too. "You're amazing, Jack. Truly amazing. And, yes, I can definitely turn that into a feast."

Greta's eyes were so wide you'd think Jack had performed a magic trick right in front of her. Part of me shared her sense of wonder.

• • •

Maggie and I got the goose and potatoes cooking, improvising as we went to get our limited cooking implements to do the job, but with a gift like this, nothing was going to stop us from putting on a wonderful meal. Jack had apparently done more than traded for our Christmas dinner; he'd also managed to procure a small wooden game that involved pegs and dice for Greta. Delighted at the unexpected gift, she wanted to play immediately. Wordlessly she held out the game to Jack and let longing shine from her eyes.

I had to laugh. "For someone who doesn't speak, she certainly knows how to get her way."

Maggie giggled, a girlish sound that spoke clearly of her excitement over our ad hoc Christmas. "She's never had a problem with getting what she wants. She's quiet but efficient. Two days and she's already got Jack wrapped around her little finger."

I had to agree as I watched Jack, sprawled on the floor on his side, teaching Greta how to play. Enchanted by the sight, I turned back to Maggie. She was caught by the sight that had amused me, but her expression told of emotions far more complicated. I turned away, not wanting to intrude on the privacy of her thoughts.

Our Christmas meal was indeed something to remember. It was as though, at least for a few hours, we'd agreed to suspend all thought, all worry. Instead we laughed, told stories, savored every bite of the sumptuous meal.

"Tell me what you'd be doing today if you were back home." Maggie's voice was soft and relaxed, echoing her expression.

I sat back and tried to remember, to think of what I'd be doing at this moment if I were back in New York. "Christmas Eve always takes place at my parents' house. I'd go over in the late afternoon, and we'd have a meal, like this one but not as special," I said, winking at Greta. "We'd sit in front of a fire and exchange gifts." I could almost feel the roar and crackle of the fire as I spoke. My cheeks flushed with heat from the fire and my soul content, replete from the unyielding tradition. Since the first Christmas I could remember it had always been like that. Like a time out from life, from the family friction. It was just good. I felt a sudden pang of homesickness so strong it made me ache. Half a world away, I wished for a moment that I could be there.

"Your mother and I spent a lot of Christmases together when we were young," Jack said to Greta, his eyes dark and unreadable in the flickering candlelight. "Everyone would gather at my house, until it felt like not another person could fit. The house would be hot and full of food. Mostly Italian. And there would be games between the cousins, loud debates between the uncles about everything from politics to sports."

Maggie grinned. "And then there'd be the food competition. You'd have to be so careful filling your plate, making sure that you didn't take more of one aunt's food than another's. You couldn't show favoritism, or there'd be trouble."

Jack laughed, continuing the story. "And you'd have to start claiming fullness way before you were done eating because they would just keep filling and filling your plate: 'You're a growing boy. You need to eat,'" he said, raising his voice and doing a fairly credible impression of his mother. "By the time we finally escaped from the food-wielding women we were so stuffed we could barely move."

Greta looked and pointed at the little piles of goose meat and potatoes on her plate. We all looked over in time to see Maggie spooning a little more onto Greta's plate, almost automatically.

Jack pointed. "You're doing it too. You've become one of them!"

Maggie dropped the spoon with a clatter and her face went white, staring at her hand as though she'd seen a ghost. "It's true. I'm turning into an Italian mama." She looked shell-shocked at the realization, but she managed a stuttering laugh.

"And after the food and the fire, my father would read the Christmas story out loud from the book of Luke," I said, coming to Maggie's rescue by telling Greta about the rest of the Christmas Eve traditions in my family.

Jack nodded. "Sounds just like our Christmas Eves. And it sounds like a perfect way to end our evening too." He looked to Maggie, and she nodded, rose, and went to the back bedroom. When she returned, she had an old, worn Bible in her hands. She passed it to Jack.

He flipped through the pages for a moment until he found what he was looking for. "And it came to pass in those days, that there went out a decree from Caesar Augustus that all the world should be taxed . . ."

I listened to the familiar words and closed my eyes, imagining myself back home, spending Christmas Eve with my family. As he continued to read about a virgin giving birth in a stable I opened my eyes and saw for the first time that these three, despite circumstances and the issues that stood between them, already looked like a family. I smiled, then let my eyes drift closed and listened to the story once more.

Chapter 37

THE NEXT MORNING I left before anyone else was awake. It was Christmas morning, but I couldn't imagine a more cheerless scene. It was cold out again and overcast. So far Berlin seemed to me a city made up entirely of shades of grey.

I'd asked Jack to ask around about St. Martin's church, and he'd been able to get more information in five minutes than I'd found through yesterday's adventure. I made the long trek to the church, where I hoped I'd still be able to find Father Heinrich Neumann. I followed the directions Jack had procured to the letter, careful to stay away from debris piles as I picked my way through the ruined streets.

The church was located in the British sector, and Maggie had just shaken her head when I told her where I wanted to go. I had the feeling that it didn't bode well, but I hadn't asked any questions, I'd just set out, determined to find it.

I knew I'd arrived because the church was the only one in the vicinity, but the sight of it dashed my hopes. The church was a sad mix of destruction and beauty. Built of cut stone it had huge windows with only shatters of stained glass left gaping around the edges. Twin spires lined the building like masks of comedy and tragedy, one strong and beautiful as a fairy tale, the other clawed and gutted with rough edges and blackened stone.

There was no hope that it was still in use. Most of the roof was gone, and it shook me to see the echo of something that had been so beautiful but that now resembled a nightmare of destruction and flame.

I tore my eyes away from the bombed-out building and turned to see the rest of the street. Several buildings had also sustained damage, but nothing as devastating as this one. I saw an old woman sweeping her stairs, and I crossed to her. I hoped that my lack of German wouldn't hamper me as much this time.

I came to stand at the base of her step. She heard me approach and turned to glare. I didn't let her scowl deter me. I turned and pointed to the church then turned back to her. "Heinrich Neumann?" I tried to use body language to get my question across.

Her face folded into even deeper scowl lines, and she turned her back to me. Undaunted I said the name again. "Heinrich Neumann?" I tried another tack. "Vater Neumann?"

She turned back to me and pointed down the street, spitting guttural words at me that I had no hope of translating. I looked in the direction she pointed, but could only see more homes and a few large apartment buildings several blocks away.

I turned in that direction with the idea of finding someone else and trying again. After about half a block the woman called out something. I turned and saw her gesture to the left. I turned and saw that next to the destroyed church was a small building, a house, built simply but with the same materials as the church. I realized that it had probably been built as accommodations for the priest. A manse of sorts. This building seemed to be undamaged.

I shifted the package I held from hand to hand. Curiosity clawed at me, but that very desire to know why my mother had asked me to find this man also made me wary. Perhaps it would have been better to refuse this job, to keep the relationship, which was already complicated and fraught with undercurrents and riptides, as simple as possible. I couldn't imagine what could really go wrong with this little mystery my mother had handed me, but experience had taught me to tread carefully with anything that involved two Fortune women.

I turned to see if the old woman who'd given me directions was still there, but the street appeared to be deserted. Taking a deep breath, I stepped forward and crossed to the little manse.

The door was solid wood, dark with age and medieval looking with black forged hinges. I straightened my hat and smoothed the edges of my thick woolen coat before forcing myself to knock on the door.

I banged, rapping my knuckles against the wood, wondering if the noise would even penetrate and carry through into the house. After a moment I knocked again, but it was several more seconds before the door swung open.

A low creaking sharpened my attention, and as the door opened I saw an old man, hunched and white haired but wearing the vestments that told me this could possibly be the man I was looking for.

I cleared my throat. "Vater Neumann?"

His eyes widened slightly at my non-Germanic accent, but he nodded and stepped aside from the doorway to let me inside.

The entranceway was much warmer than the frigid cold outside, and I felt my body relax slightly as the air buffeted my chilled skin.

The man before me had a crown of white hair and papery skin that looked both soft and brittle. Eyebrows white as snow with thick long hairs made his face soft and approachable. I cleared my throat again and took a second to hope that this was the man I was looking for and that he spoke English.

"Are you Heinrich Neumann?"

He nodded. "Do I know you Fraulein?"

His English was excellent with only the barest hint of Teutonic harshness at the end of his words. I shook my head. "No, you don't. I'm visiting Berlin and was asked to find you and deliver something to you."

His eyebrows rose. "Visiting Berlin. It is not a good place to visit these days, I think."

I had to smile. "I'm not here on vacation, just passing through."

He nodded, and I saw a flash of understanding in his eyes. He was no stranger to evasive answers.

"We shall have tea, and you can tell me why you've come." It wasn't a question, it was a gentle shepherding order, and I knew better than to argue with the seemingly frail man. I had a feeling that he usually got his way.

I followed him through the house. We walked along a long corridor to the very back of the house and entered a kitchen of sorts. If the house had been built two hundred years ago, then the kitchen looked as though it hadn't changed or been updated since. There was a large fireplace against one wall, an open larder, and a metal-handled water pump with a basin under it. There was also a long, rough wooden table with benches on either side of it. I slipped in, sat down, and took a look around.

It had probably been a blessing not to have an updated kitchen, as everything here still worked, despite the lack of electricity and the poor conditions in the city. Father Neumann filled a cast-iron kettle with water from the pump, then hung it on a hook over the roaring fire.

I slipped off my gloves and shoved them into my coat pockets, enjoying the intense heat pumping out from the fire. Father Neumann said nothing as he moved around the room, bringing a teapot to the table and pulling out a box of tea.

I set the package I'd been carrying on the bench next to me, not ready just yet to get into the crux of my visit.

He bustled around the kitchen, retrieving cups and saucers. By the time he had everything ready I could see the water steaming in its kettle.

Within a few minutes he had the water poured, the tea was steeping, and he was finally still, sitting on the bench across from me. For such a fragile-looking man he seemed very capable. He looked as though carrying the heavy water kettle would be too much for him, but he'd waved away my offer of help with impatient and surprisingly capable hands.

He poured tea into my cup and pushed it across the table toward me. As he did, the sleeve of his vestment pulled up and I saw blue numbers along his forearm. I tried not to stare, but he caught the direction of my gaze.

"Were you in a camp?" I asked. I found it hard to believe that this fragile old man, who looked to be eighty if he was a day, had survived a concentration camp.

"Near the end, yes," was all he said.

I let the topic slide, knowing that it probably wasn't polite to ask him more about his experiences. I needed to get down to business. "I was asked to bring this to you," I said and handed the box across the table to him.

Surprise colored his eyes, but he reached out for the gleaming box. He stroked the smooth wood with shaky fingers. I kept a close eye on his face, monitoring his expression when he saw the delicate box.

His eyes shifted from mildly interested to surprise to something like sorrow. Their final shift was to joy. He ran his fingers along the underside of the box, caressing it as though it were silk. I thought I saw the sheen of tears for a second, and I reached out to touch his hand.

"This box means something to you?"

He ran his fingers along the line of the Japanese woman's face on the wood and smiled. He looked up. "How is my dear Elanor?" he asked.

I sat back, surprised. "Elanor Fortune?" I asked, already knowing that's who he was talking about.

He didn't answer. Then, "I haven't seen her in years."

"You know my mother?" The words slipped out, and I could have kicked myself for losing my professional distance. I'd never intended to confess that his Elanor was my mother.

He looked closely at me, cataloguing my features it seemed. "Yes, you must be her daughter. Alexandra, correct?"

I nodded, uncomfortable now. I shifted in my seat and waited for him to tell me how he knew my mother and how he knew of me.

Instead his rheumy brown eyes seemed to go even farther away, as though lost in the past.

I cleared my throat, and when that didn't get his attention, I spoke softly. "Can you tell me, Father, how you know my mother?"

Chapter 38

THE OLD MAN was silent for several long moments, his fingers playing with the box, running fingers along the top, the sides, as though memorizing its texture. "Your mother has told you nothing about this box?" he asked. He looked up at me, his eyes finally off the box.

"Nothing." I was a little surprised by the serious tone of his voice. I wasn't sure how I'd imagined this meeting going, but the strong emotions in this priest's eyes made me a little uncomfortable.

"This box has saved lives. So many lives," he said.

I remained silent, waiting for him to explain.

"I met your mother years and years ago in France. I was staying with a friend. I was on a little holiday. Just taking a few days away from the daily struggles of church life. It must have been 1938 or '39. It was after Kristallnacht, and the whole world was a little stunned at the anti-Semitic sentiment that seemed to possess Germany overnight." He rubbed his fingers along the inside of his forearm.

"I do remember that your mother was visiting there as well. My friend was a relation of hers. We spent several enjoyable evenings debating the state of Germany, the mindset of its people, and fear throughout much of the world at the rantings of Adolf Hitler. Your mother was a worthy debater and had many insights into the reaction of European leaders. I enjoyed her company a great deal.

"When my holiday days were up, I left, feeling refreshed and watered. I confess that I never expected to hear from your mother again after that. But a few months later I found her on my doorstep."

I leaned forward, trying to imagine my mother, as I knew her, showing up at this man's door, uninvited.

"I was surprised to see her but invited her in for tea." He paused. "In fact, seeing you on my doorstep had a slight tinge of déjà vu to it. Now I know why." He shook his head before continuing. "We sat down to tea and discussed life, politics, philosophy. It was similar to our discussions in France, but I felt as though there was more of a seeking quality to this discussion. As though she were probing and testing me so subtly that I started to wonder if I was turning into a paranoid old man." He laughed, and I smiled politely.

"Anyway, after several hours of stimulating conversation she stood. 'Thank you Father. I've gotten the answers I came for.' I walked her to the door, bemused at the strange visit. As she was about to leave she made a simple request. 'Father, would you hear my confession before I go?'"

I started at this. My mother was firmly Protestant. There was no way on earth I could imagine her saying these words. I narrowed my eyes at the old man.

He just laughed, then continued with his story. "It didn't matter that it was by now well into the evening, I said, 'Of course,' and I led her over to the church. It was clear from the minute we got there that she'd never been inside a Catholic church before, never mind given confession, but she gamely followed me and within minutes we were ensconced in my very familiar role as Father Confessor.

"But your mother was far from a typical confessor. She started talking as soon as we were both in the booth, words that at first shocked me, words that changed my life."

I tried to imagine this scene, but it was almost impossible.

"She started by telling me that she was a Protestant, but that she knew that nothing she said within the confines of the booth could be repeated. I assured her that this was the case, then she went on. She told me that she, along with many in the Western world, was greatly troubled by the atrocities that were happening at the hands of the Nazis. Word was leaking out about the formation of the first concentration camps, about atrocities that were already being committed. She asked if I thought that the barbaric, subhuman treatment of the Jews was wrong. Now we had already spent hours discussing this over tea, but I felt a different, deeper urgency in this question. I told her that I believed it was a sin against God to treat any of His people that way.

"That must have been enough to assure her, because that's when she told me why she'd really come."

I took a deep breath and waited for him to continue.

"Elanor was a well-traveled woman, with friends and connections all over the world. She told me that she had a contact who worked at a passport office in Spain. This person had the ability to provide false Spanish passports to people who needed out of Germany, but she needed a contact within Germany to handle the distribution of the passports. Your mother asked me to be one link in a chain of people who worked to get men, women, and children out of Germany and out of the reach of the Gestapo."

I shook my head. "My mother wouldn't—"

The old man interrupted me, putting his hand over mine on the table. "Forgive me if I'm wrong, but I think one of the reasons you're here with me today is because you don't know very much about your mother at all." I tried to say something, but he sent me a hard look and my mouth closed, swallowing the denial. "Listen to my story and find out who your mother really was." I nodded, swallowing the lump in my throat.

"She told me that she would bring the passports from Spain to Germany, give them to me, and I would take care of the distribution. I sat there in my confessional, stunned. I knew there was an underground, an organized resistance to the plans of the German government, but I hadn't ever thought of myself as any more than a neutral party. But I hesitated for only a moment. While passing out fraudulent passports was deceitful and wrong, standing by and watching as Jews were abused and eventually slaughtered was a far worse sin."

He moved his hand from on top of mine and reached over to grab the wooden box. I watched as he ran a finger along the top of it, sliding a strip of the seemingly seamless wood back half an inch. He then pulled another strip crossways, opening yet another gap. I watched, startled, as through the process of a dozen or so moves he opened the box to reveal two envelopes inside.

I sat back, and my breath huffed out. He looked up and smiled. "It's a puzzle box. We probably used a dozen or so different ones over the years. It was mighty complicated trying to remember how to open each one of them." He confessed, "I've been afraid since the minute I saw it today that my forgetful old mind wouldn't remember how." He grinned, crinkling his face into deeper wrinkles. "But I've still got the touch."

I smiled but couldn't keep from reaching into the box to pull out the envelopes that were inside.

My mother's elegant script was on both. One was addressed to Father Heinrich and one was addressed to Alexandra. With trembling fingers I pulled them both out. I handed the priest his and ran my fingers along the edges of mine. It was sealed, but I couldn't quite bring myself to open it just yet. Father Neumann saw my hesitation. "I shall just go read this in the privacy of my room. You go ahead and make yourself at home, have another cup of tea, and find out why your mother sent you all the way here to meet me." With that he turned and headed out of the kitchen.

I set the letter down on the table in front of me. I closed my eyes and for a second tried to put aside everything that the old man had just told me. I felt a little unstable, a little dizzy. I took a sip of my tea then picked up the letter. How was it possible that my mother had done all of this without me knowing anything about it? Perhaps the priest was wrong, or perhaps he was exaggerating. That's why they called tall tales war stories. They always tended to get bigger and more dramatic upon retelling.

I let myself sink into that explanation for a second before logic intervened. I had watched his face as he spoke. I'd seen the tattooed numbers on his arm. This was not a man who needed to, or would, exaggerate to make himself appear to be a hero. Whatever he said was going to be the truth. I could feel it in my bones.

I slid my nail under the flap of the envelope, but hesitated. I knew that as soon as I read this, things were going to change between my mother and me. And I wasn't sure I was ready. I didn't enjoy the way things were between us, but I didn't necessarily want to change them either. I didn't want to see my mother in any way but as I'd always known her. And, selfishly, I didn't want my view of her to change because, like a ripple in a pond, I knew it was going to change my understanding of myself as well.

"Stop being a coward Allie," I muttered to myself. Taking a steadying breath I tore the flap and yanked out the sheet of paper.

Alexandra,

Well I suppose if you're reading this letter Father Neumann is alive and still sharp as ever as he's the only one who could have opened the box.

I'm not sure how much he's told you about what this box was used for in the past, but given Heinrich's propensity for talking, I'm guessing that he's told you a lot. Father Neumann is a hero, he helped save countless lives before and during the war. As you know, living in Berlin and providing false passports to Jews was a risky proposition. Not to put too fine a point on it, but if he'd been found out, the Gestapo would have made an example out of him. He risked much to do what was right.

And I guess that was my point in asking you to deliver this box to Father Neumann. I wanted you to see, to understand that doing the right thing has a price. I lost track of Heinrich during the war, but I do know that the Spanish passport official who provided the passports was arrested and I never heard from her again.

Some of the families, some of the children we provided passports for, were caught. I know some of them were killed.

Over the past several years I've seen you search, I've seen the circles beneath your eyes from too many nights of lost sleep over a man who didn't come home.

David isn't coming home. He chose to fight for what was right and he paid a price for that choice, and I pray that maybe soon you'll find that it's time for you to let him go. To stop searching and stop wondering, and just remember him as a hero who did what he needed to do.

I wish I could make it easier, I wish you would find some man who would sweep you off your feet and make you happy, but it's not up to me. It's up to you to move forward, and I truly hope that someday soon you'll be able to.

If nothing else, I'll pack up my grandmother's wedding veil and leave it in the attic in case it's ever needed. And not as a tablecloth.

It's time to let go of David as the man you used to know and instead, it's time for you to accept that he's one of the heroes who didn't come home.

I love you Allie.
Mother

Chapter 39

I TOOK A CIRCUITOUS route back to Maggie's apartment, dogged by the hair-raising feeling of being watched. I couldn't spot anyone following me, so I tried to convince myself that I was just being paranoid. Still, I was relieved when I finally made it back to Maggie's apartment. I would be glad to get inside, out of the open. In fact, I'd just be glad to get out of this city altogether. The feeling of oppression was so strong that I felt almost suffocated by it.

I checked to make sure no one was watching before I slipped into the dank stairwell and entered Maggie's apartment. I looked around the room and didn't see anyone. I wondered if perhaps Maggie was still sleeping.

I crept up to the bedroom door and prepared to knock. A sound came from inside the room and it brought all of my instincts roaring to life. I don't know what tipped me off, but I knew, immediately, that something was wrong.

Throwing caution aside, I reached for the doorknob and threw the door open. For a moment I couldn't see anything in the dimness, but it was only for a moment. Then what I did see sent a spurt of cold fear through my belly.

Maggie was sitting on one of the wooden chairs, her arms pulled behind her. Her ankles were bound together, and she was gagged. Despite the cloth in her mouth, a muffled yell came from her throat. I rushed to her side and saw great fat tears rolling down her cheeks. I pulled the wad of cloth from her mouth and immediately she tried to speak. It took her several seconds for the words to come out coherently. "Greta's gone. They've taken her."

She choked out the words again as I untied her arms and legs. "Where did they take her? Who took her?" I asked the questions as fast as my brain came up with them.

"Two men, Soviets I think. They came in here minutes after you left and told me that they'd kill me if I didn't hand over the documents to them. I told them that I didn't have them here, and they took Greta. They told me that I had until midnight to get them, and if I didn't, they'd kill her." Maggie could hardly get the words out.

"It's okay. We'll get her back." I murmured the words over and over, as much to convince myself as to soothe Maggie. The thought of Greta in the hands of the Soviets made me go cold all over.

"I need you to tell me exactly when and where we're supposed to bring them the documents," I said, trying to clamp down on my fear and assume my normal role as impartial investigator.

Maggie took a deep breath. Her red hair had come loose from its efficient bun, and her eyes were wild. "They said I had until midnight tonight to get the documents. I was to bring them to

Oberbaum Bridge and hand them over there. If I did, Greta wouldn't be harmed." The last words held hints of fear in her voice.

I opened my mouth to ask the next logical question but was stopped when I heard a noise coming from the other room. My breath backed up in my throat, and I gestured to Maggie to remain silent.

I crept to the door and peered out. My breath came out in a sigh when I saw it was Jack, back from the American sector. I relaxed from my crouched position and strode out to where he stood.

"We have a big problem." I didn't soften the announcement, and I watched as Jack set his hat on the table and turned to me.

"What happened?"

As Maggie came into the room, and Jack's gaze moved from me to her, Maggie clenched her hands in front of her, twining her fingers, twisting and pulling.

"They've got Greta. They're going to kill her if I don't give them the documents."

I watched Jack pale. "How fast can you get them?" he asked.

Maggie's hands trembled as she pushed her hair out of her face. "As soon as it's dark. It will probably take me about an hour."

"Jack, we can't just hand these papers over to the Soviets," I broke in.

He didn't even turn to look at me, keeping his

eyes on Maggie's face instead, speaking to her as though swearing an oath. "Maggie, I promise. We'll get her back, safe and sound. And I'm going to get both of you out of here." He took a step toward her.

Maggie had her arms wrapped around herself as though to hold herself together. Jack moved closer, with the assurance of someone who knows when he is needed, and enfolded her in his arms. She lay her head, unresisting, on his shoulder. There were tears in her voice when she finally spoke.

"I can't lose her too. I can't be alone again. We only have each other."

Jack pulled her closer. "We will get her back. I promise." He took a deep breath. "I'm not leaving Berlin without her."

Chapter 40

MAGGIE

NAUSEA SWIRLED through her gut as worry and fear battled for supremacy in her mind. She knew that she needed to pray, but there were no words. Instead she just closed her eyes.

She was still stunned. How could this possibly have happened again? She recalled how Cullum had looked beside her in the Jeep, his deep brown eyes, his silver and black hair, recalled the kindness that was as much a part of him as his smile, and she'd felt nothing. Faint stirrings of friendship, wailing sirens of alarm, but no stirring of reciprocated love. She'd tried to be kind as she told him that she didn't love him back. She wanted to, oh, how she wanted to. He was everything a woman could want in a man, in a husband. Just not for her.

What was wrong with her? Was there something broken inside that wouldn't, that couldn't, allow her to surrender enough to love a good man? Since the moment she'd returned to the camp she'd lain on her cot, questioning, searching her heart. Panic threatened to overtake her when all she could find was cold emptiness. She shuddered and felt tears spill down her face as her thoughts led her in circles. "You'll end up alone and unhappy," they taunted her. "You've kicked aside your chances at a happy life."

She shook her head. She still hadn't found what she was looking for. The thought screamed through her head. What was she searching for? What had brought her halfway across the world, what had forced her to walk away from a man who loved her and who she was starting to realize that she loved back?

Not what. Who.

The words slipped, fully formed, into her mind. Maggie shoved herself off the cot and paced the small tent, trying to sort out her thoughts. Trying to understand, to grasp something big, an understanding that seemed just out of reach.

Who was she searching for? The question flittered through her mind, and the answer lay somewhere just beyond her.

Frustrated, Maggie blew out a breath. The lapse in concentration allowed the outside world to intrude. Just outside her tent she heard the familiar sounds of an impending shift change. She checked her watch. Ten minutes until she was due in the OR.

Out of time, she wanted to scream in frustration as she pulled out a clean uniform and pulled it on. The tendrils of whatever profound realization she'd been reaching for had danced out of her reach. Fluttering away like ribbons in a breeze.

The OR was extraordinarily busy that night, and Maggie was glad for busy hands and an occupied mind. She kept her mind on her work and kept her eyes from meeting Cullum's. Shelling had moved dangerously close to the evac hospital, so close that the concussion of the blasts had set the lights above the operating tables swaying like rowboats in a gale. Every few seconds a burst of noise sounded as though bombs would be landing on top of them next. Everyone was mostly used to it, but the fact that the entire surgical team was wearing helmets in the operating room was a testament to the danger.

Maggie held out a scalpel to Cullum just as another shell burst shook the tent and made the lights flicker. Another burst followed almost immediately, accompanied by a screeching, ripping sound. Her head turned in time to see the board that held a sterile sheet forming the operating room come crashing down from the ceiling. She called out a warning, but a split second too late. It hammered down on the back of the anesthesiologist's neck. He fell forward, into the table, knocking into the patient before sliding, unconscious, to the floor.

Maggie dropped the instrument she held and reached out to steady the patient. One of the other nurses screamed. Cullum muttered under his breath as a sudden spurt of blood shot up from the patient's chest.

"Team, focus. Focus on the patient." He held his hands out for forceps, she handed them to him, and he clamped off the bleed before shouting, "Get medics in here. Dr. Miller has been injured." He didn't appear to ever pull his attention away from what he was doing, and Maggie forced herself to concentrate along with him even as she fought the urge to check on Dr. Miller. Cullum's eyes lifted from the patient's chest for a second to call out, "This is a sterile area. No one comes in here unless they're scrubbed in and sterile." She turned to see the medics shoving themselves into boiled scrubs.

"Nurse O'Shayne, our patient is down here. Pay attention."

Maggie flushed and returned her gaze instantly to where it should have been. She could have kicked herself for allowing herself to be distracted.

She worked next to Cullum, trying to make up for her lapse, not looking up, even as the medics came in and started working on the still unconscious doctor at her feet. She didn't look as she felt them roll him onto a stretcher, didn't pay attention to anything other than the operation in progress on the table, until she felt something wet on her hand. She looked down and saw blood seeping from a long cut across her left hand. Looking at the operating table she realized she must have cut herself on the scalpel she'd been holding when Dr. Miller went down. The cut wasn't very deep, but blood was about to start dripping down onto the patient. She took a step back from the table.

"What are you doing, Nurse O'Shayne?" Cullum's voice was hard, but he never looked up at her.

"I got cut when Dr. Miller went down. I'm about to start bleeding in the patient."

Cullum moved his gaze, took in the cut, and apparently agreed with her assessment that it wasn't too bad. "Scrub out, Nurse O'Shayne. Bandage your hand, change your scrubs, and then come back as soon as you're sterile again."

She stepped away from the table, feeling guilty despite the fact that she'd done nothing wrong. Maggie watched as the medics hauled the anesthesiologist out of the operating room and took him to an exam table. One of the off-duty doctors had been summoned and was dealing with the newest casualty.

She went back to her tent, changed, bandaged her hand, and took a deep breath to get her focus back.

She started back for the OR tent. The booming of the artillery in the dark reminded her of thunderstorms back home. It was comforting in a way. The occasional burst of light provided illumination as she made her way through the darkened camp.

She continued walking, quickening her step in order to get back before the operation was over, but she stumbled at the huge boom of a shell hitting a tent twenty feet from where she was standing.

They'd hit the hospital. Maggie's mind reeled. This was a safe zone. The shelling had been coming closer and closer, but she'd never really believed that the enemy forces would actually attack a hospital. She turned toward the tent, ran toward it, knowing it was nursing barracks, knowing that there was a good chance there'd been people inside.

A bright light flashed, followed by the deafening sound of shells exploding mere feet away. Maggie saw the flying debris milliseconds before it hit her. She turned her face away but she felt something slice along the back of her neck, just below the rim of her helmet. Pain, screaming and hot, assaulted for a moment before she fell to the ground and awareness dimmed.

You brought me through those times, Lord, and I know that You will bring me through these too. Maggie felt the first measure of peace she'd experienced in hours.

Chapter 41

ALLIE

I WAS THE MOST objective of the group. Not
that I wasn't terrified for Greta's sake too, but I
was just the most dispassionate and able to reason.

"Okay, Maggie, you need to tell us what's in
those documents." She started to protest, pushing herself out of Jack's arms, but I overrode her.
"We have to understand what's going on here. We
can't work in the dark anymore."

Maggie chewed her lip as she considered.

We waited.

Finally she pushed herself all of the way out of
Jack's arms and put a few feet of distance between
them. "Okay, like I told you, Greta came home
with the things she'd taken off the soldier's body.
Boots, coat, gun, things like that. Everything she
thought we might be able to sell or use. And then
she pulled out this long tube-like container. It was
about a foot long and about an inch around, with a
strap that would go across a soldier's body. I'd
never seen anything like that before, so I was
curious.

"The top was held closed by a buckle, and I
undid it carefully, having no idea what was inside.
I was worried that it was some sort of weapon I
didn't recognize, but when a sheet of rolled-up

paper slid out, I was relieved that it wasn't dangerous." Maggie laughed, but it was a bitter laugh. "How could I have known that that little sheet of paper was more dangerous than a live grenade would have been?" She shook her head.

"I pulled out the rolled paper and saw that it was sealed closed."

"The seal wasn't broken?" Jack interrupted, his tone sharp.

Maggie looked up. "No, the wax was definitely still intact."

He nodded and waited for her to continue.

"I was curious, so I broke the seal and read it." She paused. "For a second, I didn't understand it.

"It was a handwritten document. It had a few sentences of writing and a list of names. It appeared that the document had been written in English, but underneath the English words, it was translated into Russian.

"My guess is that it was written by a spy within the Allied military presence here. Whoever it was must have had a very high clearance level because he listed the names and ranks of three American and British moles inside the Soviet military compound in Berlin."

Jack's breath huffed out. "This is not good news."

I shook my head. This was about spies and intelligence? That list of names would be worth a lot more than the life of one little girl, or even the lives of three adults and one little girl, to certain people.

To say nothing of what would happen to those spies within the Soviet ranks if they were found out. I shuddered at the thought.

It was silent for several minutes. I pictured the last several weeks in Maggie's life with a new understanding. She had understood, completely how this information could doom them. "You said before that trying to pass the information on ended with you being accused of the murder of two soldiers. What happened?"

Maggie sighed. "Right after finding the documents I went to the American base. I told them I needed to talk to the officer in charge. That I had information. I gave them the bare-bones details of what kind of information I had, and I was told that I would be contacted. I waited for two days before two men approached me in the street when I was shopping. They weren't the men in charge, but I was getting so nervous holding these documents that I was willing to turn them over to them, but right then, in broad daylight, someone started shooting at them, at me too I guess. The first man was killed right away. We were in a crowded street, and he was shot in front of everyone." Maggie looked shaken at the memory. "I don't really remember screaming, but I must have because the other man turned to me, saw his partner crumple to the ground, and he rushed to my side, shielding my body with his, urging me to run. He steered me out of the street, and we ran, looking for some sort of escape. The shooting had stopped, so he told me to wait for him and he left me hidden in an abandoned building. I waited there for hours, but he never came back. I know now that he was killed too." She shook her head.

"I was frantic but I waited until after dark to head back to our apartment. Greta was still there waiting for me. I knew that someone within the American camp must be working against them, and I also knew that they would have access to information about me, like where I lived, my name, everything. We had to leave our apartment immediately. We left almost everything behind, not that there was so much, but I had to leave my job. All of our identity papers would lead whoever wanted that information right to us, so they had to be abandoned too.

"That night, we slept in the stairwell of an abandoned building in the British sector, and I traded three pairs of wool socks for a pencil, paper, envelopes, and stamps. I wrote you," she turned to Jack, "that letter and paid an old woman to take it to the French sector to send it for me. I wrote another letter a few days later and posted it from a different location, hoping that at least one of them would get to you. For weeks I wondered if she'd even mailed hers, if I was waiting in vain for a response to a letter that had never been sent, or that they'd both been stopped from leaving the country by censors."

She took a big breath. "We've been hiding ever since. I discovered a few days after the two men were killed that I'd been accused of the murder. And now you see why I can't go to the Americans, why I have to get out of the city."

Neither one of us said anything. I was still trying to process the information.

"And now someone has Greta," she said, tears clogging up her voice. "I want to do the right thing, I want to make sure that this information doesn't get into the wrong hands, but I have to keep Greta safe. That is my ultimate objective, and I can't fail her."

I nodded, understanding, wishing I could promise that everything was going to turn out all right.

"How do you think they found me?" she asked.

"The better question is, how long have they known where you are? Do they know who we are? Do they know you're not alone?" I said.

Jack took a step forward. "We have to assume that they know we're here. And I think we have to hope that they don't know who we are."

Chapter 42

MAGGIE

THERE. THEY NOW knew everything she did. Maggie breathed a sigh of relief and shut the door of the bedroom. Jack and Allie were still absorbing the information she'd just shared in the main room.

She'd needed to get away for a moment to try to get her courage back. Telling the story had reminded her once again of how very much she had to lose. It had been such a burden carrying these secrets, but at least she'd finally been able to tell them, to name out loud the monster she was running from.

It couldn't be much past noon yet, six hours at least before she could leave the apartment. More if she wanted to wait until full dark. Obviously someone knew where she was, but if she traveled in daylight, someone else who was looking for her might spot her, take her into custody, and then she would miss the meeting. Nothing, nothing could stop her from making that meeting and making the exchange for Greta.

So she could only wait. She sat down against the wall, let her head tilt back, and stared at the ceiling. *God, why is all this happening? I don't understand. We were so close. We only had to make it through another day and one way or another Greta was going to get out of Berlin.* With or without her, but Greta'd be safe.

She crossed her arms over her chest and tried to still the shaking in her hands.

Maggie lifted her head at the sound of the door creaking open. Jack waited at the threshold until she waved him in.

He took two steps into the room, then shut the door behind him. "You holding it together?" Concern etched his face.

"By the very tips of my fingers." She took a deep breath. "I'm going to go crazy waiting for nightfall. All I can see in my mind is how terrified Greta must be."

He crossed the room, leaned his back against the wall, and slid down beside her. Maggie felt her breath catch at his nearness.

"Talk to me instead of focusing on the unknown."

Maggie hesitated. She did not have any idea where to start.

"There are five years' worth of experiences that I know nothing about. Tell me the best and the worst things that have happened in those years. That should give you somewhere to begin," he said with a gentle smile.

"The best? Undoubtedly Greta. Finding her was me finally realizing that my life had a purpose. It changed me."

"And the worst?" he asked.

How much should she tell him? Things between them were as stable as quicksand, and maybe the truth would shift something. It could change things between them in a way that could never go back.

MILITARY HOSPITAL, VIRGINIA

Two months of convalescing had left Maggie desperate. The sheer tedium of days filled by nothing but lying in a hospital bed was enough to drive her mad. She remembered little about being injured and nothing about being treated at the evac hospital. She'd woken up aboard a medical ship headed for the US. She'd been hit by something, possibly a tent pole, during the shelling attack and had been in a coma for more than three weeks. Aside from the head injury, she also had a long riverbed of a scar across the back of her neck, courtesy of a chunk of burning shrapnel. Mostly healed now, it was the most visible but least complicated injury she'd sustained.

Even after two months of recuperation she still had problems with vertigo and crippling headaches. But today she was getting out. She'd asked for permission to leave the hospital to visit family. The fact that she had no family had escaped the notice of her doctor, and she'd been granted a weekend off-base pass. Still listed as an active member of the military she had to receive permission to leave or she would be listed as AWOL. Armed with little more than a bus ticket that would take her to New York City, Maggie packed her bag of toiletries and a change of clothes and was driven to the nearest bus station.

The trip from Virginia to New York was long, and the constant bumping brought Maggie's ever-present headache to roaring life, but the journey gave her time to think about what she was doing.

She didn't bother even trying to fool herself. There was only one reason to go back to New York. It wasn't her home, she had no ties left; the only thing it held was the one person she'd walked away from but hadn't been able to forget. Something in her, something strong and a little frightening, pulled at her, wouldn't let her rest. She still hadn't found what she was looking for, who she was looking for. Nothing in the past year had brought her closer to where she needed to be, had taught her what she needed to know. Almost since the instant she'd regained consciousness she'd felt like there was a sucking wound in her chest. Torn open and bleeding, it was no longer a matter of wandering until she found something to fill it; she was going to die if she couldn't find what it was her soul was searching for.

She slept fitfully on the bus, doing her best to ignore the chatter around her. Most of the talk was of the war overseas, and it made her head pound harder to even try to sort it all out. When they finally pulled into their final stop in the city, she breathed a sigh of relief. She'd made it this far.

New York was the same as she remembered. It was midwinter, the frigid greyness a desperate shock to a body used to the African sun. Being outside in the screaming cold cleared her head somewhat, but it also tightened all of her muscles, bringing on the shivers. She wrapped her arms around herself and was glad for the heavy felted wool uniform coat she'd been given back at the hospital. She hadn't wanted to take it as she wanted to stay inconspicuous on the streets, but there were many people in uniform striding through the streets. She was just one of many.

As she looked around the familiar sights of the city where she'd grown up, it felt like it had been decades, not mere months, since she'd been here. Stopping at a lunch counter she grabbed a quick bowl of soup and a hot dog. The combination had provoked a raised eyebrow from the waitress, but as soon as she'd seen a hot dog on the menu she'd needed to have one. The taste of summer and sunshine and home.

For the first time she felt as if she was home. Tears stung her eyes, and she looked down at her plate until the whip of emotion stilled. The longing to see Jack, always present in the background, swelled until it was the only thing she could think, see, and feel. She needed to find him. Shoving enough money down on the counter to pay for her half-eaten lunch, Maggie turned and headed out back onto the street. A subway entrance was only a few blocks away, and she picked up her pace until she was running. Ignoring the hammering in her skull, she whipped down the stairs, headed underground, Brooklyn-bound.

The old neighborhood looked exactly the same. The same brick houses that said more about pride in family and hard work than they did about money. The streets were full of snow, no doubt recent as there were still untouched sections, yet to be trampled by games of ball or sleds. Despite the fact that it was the long way around, Maggie stopped by her old house first. The one she'd shared with her parents for the first fifteen years of her life. She knew the family that lived there now, or who had a year ago, and she knew they were carrying on the tradition of laughter and love that her parents had started in that home. It brought a mixture of sadness and nostalgia, as it always did, but she forced herself to keep walking and not to get sucked into memories of the distant past.

The home where Jack's parents still lived was another block and a half down the street. She stopped in front of their stoop, unable to go to the door and knock. Jack hadn't lived in this house for years, but a sense of him still lingered. Memories flooded her, taking her breath away.

She forced herself to keep walking. The house where she'd lived in the years since her parents died was only a little ways down the sidewalk. Similar to all of the other houses, it had sheltered her in the years when she'd felt nothing more than alone. A feeling that had never entirely gone away. The only times it had receded far enough for her to almost forget were the times she'd spent with Jack.

Resting her hand on the frozen iron railing Maggie took a deep breath before finding the courage necessary to mount the cement stairs and knock on the door.

The door opened before she was ready for it. "Zia."

Italian for aunt, it was what she'd called Elodia Marculi since the day she'd moved in. "I'm back."

"You came back? And she never told me?" The fury in Jack's voice gave Maggie a chill and put a hitch in the tale. Remembering it as though it had just happened, she put her hand over Jack's to still him and continued.

Zia invited her in for coffee after getting over the initial shock of seeing her wayward adopted niece back home. Maggie entered, absorbing the familiar smell of Italian cooking and strong coffee. Midafternoon, Zia was the only one home, and that suited Maggie's purposes perfectly.

After they'd sat down to cannoli and their hot drinks, Maggie filled Zia in on her experiences in Africa. She glossed over the injury that brought her back, telling the older woman simply that she'd suffered a severe concussion and still had problems with dizziness and headaches.

"And I got a weekend pass to leave the base, so I decided to come back and see how everyone here is doing." It was more or less the truth. She'd come to see how one person in particular was doing.

Zia stared at her as though she could read Maggie's thoughts. She shifted her gaze to the coffee cups and moved to refill them both from the carafe. "Everyone is well. Joseph and Marco have both enlisted. They will be going overseas in the next few months," she said of her two oldest sons. Pride was evident in her voice, but Maggie couldn't stop the rush of sadness at the idea of Joe or Marco being one of the endless string of soldiers she'd helped to piece back together. Pushing the thought aside, she forced a smile.

"You must be very proud."

"I am. And of Jack as well. He is serving his country here, through the FBI, and he's getting married. His mother is thrilled. A son to be proud of." Zia picked up the plate of cannoli and offered Maggie another.

It was all Maggie could do not to flinch. She felt like the sucking hole in her chest had just been ripped wide open.

Jack's hand tightened on hers. "It was a lie. I was never going to marry anyone else."

"Looking back, I can see she was only trying to protect you from me."

"She was protecting me from the only thing in the world I really wanted. The only thing I needed."

"And she was keeping me from what I wanted, but indirectly she was leading me to what I needed."

She'd left Zia's as soon as she could make her excuses. She made her way back to the subway, not seeing the neighborhood this time, not seeing anything, aware of only one thing. Jack was gone too. Every single person in her life that she'd ever cared about was gone. She was totally alone.

She took the subway back to where she'd come from. She had no thoughts, no plan of what she was going to do other than to get back to the bus station and get on a bus that would take her away from this place. Away from this place that should have been home but that was empty for her.

The numbness began to wear off as she stepped off the subway. Slowly, grasping the rail for support and balance, Maggie climbed the steps and emerged up onto the street, into the light.

With as much care as someone aged or infirmed, Maggie made her way toward the bus station. Slow shuffling steps, made instinctively, gave her mind the leeway it needed to concentrate fully on everything she'd lost. Everything that was missing from her life, from inside her. How had she gotten to this point? How had she not been able to see that Jack was what she was looking for, that piece of her that had always been missing?

A shadow broke her concentration. "Are you all right, ma'am?" Through pain-clouded eyes Maggie saw a man in uniform approach her. He moved to within a foot of her and laid his hand on her arm. "Are you all right? Do you need help, ma'am?" he asked again.

Maggie shook her head. "I don't need help," she said, unable to say that she was all right.

The man smiled at her. "I wouldn't presume to call

you a liar, ma'am, but you look like you do need a little help. How about just a cup of coffee and a place to sit down for a while?"

Maggie forced herself to look at this stranger, his voice light and kind. His uniform wasn't familiar at first, but after a second it came to her. He was with the Salvation Army. He looked to be between forty-five and fifty, and he had the kindest eyes Maggie thought she'd ever seen. The sympathy and caring in them finally unleashed the tears she'd been holding back.

At a complete loss for control Maggie just cried as the man led her off the street and up the stairs into a church. The church had stained-glass windows and dark wooden pews, not a Salvation Army church, but he led her to a pew in the back, sat down next to her, and kept a hand on her back as she cried. Occasionally she could hear a whisper of words, not meant for her ears, coming from the man, but the hurt that welled to the surface drowned everything else out.

As the tears finally slowed she realized that he was praying. For her. He didn't even know her name; she was a complete stranger, and he was praying for her. Part of her wanted to slide away, get out from under his hand, out from the softly spoken words, but the man moved first. As she looked up he pulled back, slid a few inches over on the seat, and gave her some much needed space.

"Do you need to talk about it?" he asked.

She shook her head. "There's nothing you, or anyone, can do to make things better. I've made mistakes that can't be fixed, and I'm all alone. There's nothing anyone can do about that."

He smiled softly. "You're right, there's nothing I can do to make that better, but I know Someone who can. Someone who will never leave you alone and Someone who knows all your mistakes and yet forgives you anyway."

She shook her head. "That all sounds good, but I don't think even God can fix things for me now."

The man's eyes closed for a second, and when he opened them they were filled with certainty. "Ma'am, I need to tell you something." He placed his hand on her shoulder. "Right here, right now you've finally found what you've been looking for."

He chuckled. "I hope that means more to you than it does to me, but I'm absolutely certain that you are meant to hear those words."

Maggie couldn't move. Those words. The same words that had been running through her mind for most of her life, that she hadn't yet found what she was looking for—they'd been the refrain for years. How could this man who didn't know her, didn't even know her name, how could he possibly say those precise words to her? How could he know?

"I've spent the last year searching, and today I thought I was going to finally find, finally get what I've been looking for. How can you say that I've found what I've been looking for?"

His eyes were dark, the color of river stone, and to Maggie at that moment, they seemed full of answers. "God, forgiveness, and hope is what we're all looking for. Every single one of us. We wander around like blind men in a small room, bumping into people, bouncing off each other, trying to find those pieces that fit inside the deepest parts of us, the parts that cry out for something more, something eternal, something that matters. And we're all disappointed, because people can't fill those parts, they're not made to. Only God can. He fills it with His love and with His forgiveness. And in those quiet moments when you can almost grasp it, almost understand what your own soul is crying out for, it's in those moments that God is calling out to you. And I'd say that He's calling out to you right now, ma'am."

Maggie's eyes filled, and the tears began to flow again, but she had an absolute certainty in her that this man, this stranger, knew truth. Was speaking truth. To her.

"My life changed. It was both the worst and best day of my life. Because I found my direction, I found my purpose.

"Over the years I realized that if God could bring me to that street corner at that particular moment in order to tell me that He was what I'd been looking for, then He could also bring you back into my life if He wanted to." Maggie ran her hand through her hair. "I knew absolutely that I still loved you, but it seemed impossible considering that last I'd heard you were getting married. Still if it was right, I knew He could do it."

Jack's eyes were wet. "And look where I am." He reached for her hand, twining his fingers with hers.

A slow smile spread across her face. "Exactly. You're precisely where you're meant to be. And so am I."

Chapter 43

ALLIE

I COULDN'T HEAR Maggie and Jack's conversation from the living room, but I could almost feel the intensity of it through the walls. I knew we were going to have to do something, and it was likely going to be dangerous. I crossed to a box of Maggie's things high on a shelf in the corner. She'd shown me where she kept the gun Greta had taken off the Russian soldier. She kept it in case of emergencies, and I had the feeling this more than qualified. I shoved it into the pocket of my coat and said a quick prayer that I wouldn't have to use it. A few minutes later Jack came out of the bedroom looking fierce and determined. He crossed to me.

"Let's figure out how we're going to get Greta back and not let that information get into Soviet hands."

I raised my eyebrow. "You think we can do both?"

His expression was as determined as I'd ever seen it. "We're going to find a way."

It was dark with no moon, and the streets were quiet. Maggie and I left the apartment, her hair covered with a black scarf to keep from drawing attention, the details of the plan firmly stuck in our minds. We were going to win this. Get Greta back and keep that information out of Soviet hands. I was determined that we would not fail.

Maggie led the way, but we were both aware that if we were followed at this point it could lead to disaster. The walk that should have taken us fifteen minutes took more than two hours, but I was finally certain that no one could have kept us under surveillance without me being aware of it.

When I was absolutely sure, I turned my head toward Maggie and nodded. She needed no more than that to change directions and walk with purpose toward where she'd secreted the documents.

We maintained our strict code of silence. We were both focused on making sure absolutely nothing went wrong. I kept my mind focused on watching for surveillance of any kind, and I almost didn't notice as we approached a cemetery.

It looked at first just like a park of some kind, with bare, leafless tangled branches of a thick hedge proclaiming that it was winter. But when I saw the wrought metal arch that bordered a large break in the hedge I recognized the land for what it was.

Maggie crossed to the entrance, which was barred with a low gate. It wasn't enough to keep anyone out, and Maggie simply hopped over it. I did the same, taking care to make as little noise as possible.

She took a sharp left turn, and we walked past row after row of headstones. I followed behind until we reached a small building, a mausoleum. Made out of stone it looked like a miniature version of the Parthenon. Columns along the front and dark, imposing wooden doors. The mausoleum looked hundreds of years old. Maggie took a quick look around, to check yet again that no one was following us, then pulled one of the double doors open and ducked inside.

I couldn't help myself, I did the same visual sweep, even though I knew if someone had managed to follow us all the way here, then it was too late for us anyway.

I pulled the door toward me and cringed when it let out a low screech. The noise sounded like echoing thunder, and I scuttled inside, feeling the hairs on the back of my neck stand up.

I heard the door close behind me and for a moment we were sunk into blinding darkness. I fumbled at the seams of my coat, sighing in relief when my finger finally hooked on the edge of my pocket. I pulled out the flashlight I'd brought and flipped it on.

The widening circle of light it gave off made my breathing come easier. Maggie stood slightly to my left; and I handed the flashlight to her. She was the one who knew what we were doing here.

She let the beam of light sweep the entire room. I followed the path of the illumination and got the impression of several large coffin-type monuments and lots of dust.

The dust I would have known about even without the light; I smelled it, along with the stale smell of trapped air and perhaps just a little bit of mildew.

I stood still as I watched Maggie's light center on one particular monument. She walked toward it. As she left, she took the backwash of light with her, and I was once again surrounded by darkness. I took a step toward her. The light bobbled, and I heard the sound of stone scraping over stone. Within a few seconds I heard Maggie's voice. "I've got it." It was said as a whisper, but it still sounded like a trumpet in the stillness of the mausoleum.

"Let's go then," I said, trying to pitch my voice just loud enough to be heard. In the spill of light from the flashlight I saw Maggie shove a roll of paper inside her jacket. Then she led the way to the door, placed one hand on the door handle, and turned to look at me. "Ready for phase two?"

I nodded.

Maggie clicked off the light, plunging us into utter darkness before pulling the door open. Despite the fact that it was the dark of night outside, it looked brighter and more welcoming than where we'd been. I hurried out of the building, feeling my heart beating in my throat.

Phase two was going to be far more dangerous.

Chapter 44

I CHECKED MY watch, squinting to see the numbers. It was already after ten p.m. We had until midnight to get to our prearranged spot on the bridge, and we needed to take the same counter-surveillance measures on the way there that we had on the way here. It would be the end of every-thing that mattered if the documents were taken from us before the exchange.

I was thankful there was snow on the ground to keep the tapping of my heels to a minimum. The silence was so thick it was as though the city itself were holding its breath, waiting to see the out-come of the next few hours.

According to Maggie we were to meet on the car level of the Oberbaum Bridge. It was a little-used bridge these days as it linked the American sector and the Soviet sector. We would have to walk toward the center of Berlin and then pass in a semicircle from the French sector, through the

British, and on into the American. That's where the bridge meeting was going to take place.

We walked fast, ducking through side streets and keeping our eyes open for a tail. I was fairly sure we weren't being followed, but I wasn't willing to let down my guard. Too much was riding on this.

Beside me Maggie strode with quick, jerky steps, occasionally letting her hand stray to touch the front of her coat, as though she could feel the flimsy roll of paper through the fabric.

We walked for what seemed like miles through the cold, dark streets, rarely seeing a soul. As we crossed into the British sector we saw a few troops out on patrol, but we simply slid away from them, often taking long circuitous routes around, and so we never came into contact with anyone.

It was a few minutes after eleven by the time we finally crossed into the American sector. I had no idea where we were, but Maggie seemed to know exactly where she was going. We needed to be at the bridge well before the meeting time of midnight.

As we came near the bridge I saw that this was no ordinary river crossing; it was a two-level, brick behemoth that reminded me of castle walls, complete with turrets lining the top level.

There were a thousand places to hide, and the bridge itself was long. We stepped into the lower level, the vehicle level, and it looked like a tunnel that stretched way out into the darkness. We stood at the mouth of the bridge, unsure if we should go any farther in.

I watched Maggie reach inside her jacket and touch the paper again. I wondered if she knew how much she gave away with her body language. I fought not to touch the heavy gun that weighed down my pocket.

After a long silence, Maggie spoke. "I'm so afraid right now."

I absorbed her statement. What could I possibly say. It'll be all right? Well, what if it wasn't? Don't worry, this will be over soon? Things might not go the way we planned. Instead I said the only thing that was absolute truth.

"So am I."

She turned to me and nodded. "Thank you for helping me. Thank you for coming at all."

I couldn't help but smile. "I didn't want to." She looked surprised. "I was mostly trying to find a way to convince Jack not to come to Germany. Not to throw away his career with the FBI on a woman he hadn't seen in years." I paused. "And when I couldn't convince him, I decided to come with him, to keep him from getting sucked into whatever sob story you were trying to hand him." I laughed at the shocked look on her face. "Oh, I realized pretty soon after meeting you that Jack didn't really need my protection, but there's no question I was against him coming here." I stopped, curious to see how she'd respond.

"I'm not surprised. I mean, I'm surprised you're honest about it, but I'm not really surprised that you were against it. If I had been in your position, I probably would have been too."

"He was not to be dissuaded though, and good thing too."

"Yes, good thing," she murmured. "But I'm confused. Tell me what you meant about Jack giving up his career with the FBI."

I'd wondered if she'd caught that. "He had to quit his job to come here." I paused.

Maggie's eyes widened.

"He would be arrested on the spot for being here at all if he was discovered." She looked confused, so I explained. "He has a high government security clearance, and he's in a country where he has no official business being, and that country is a hotbed of selling of secrets and spying."

"You're telling me that he resigned from the FBI for me? And that he's putting himself at risk of—" She broke off, apparently not knowing what he was at risk of.

"Putting himself at risk of being tried for treason. Yes, he is. He's showing you, in every way he knows, how much he loves you."

She looked stunned. "How could he after all these years, after everything I've put him through?"

I stood in silence. Knowing exactly what it was like. In a way, she and I weren't that different. I'd spent the past eight years looking for a way to make it up to David. To take back some of the decisions I'd made back then.

But maybe it hadn't been our time either. The thought struck me as clear and strong as a hammer on a church bell, and I felt the resonance of it all the way to my toes. I knew it was time to put away the guilt and the wishing and accept that perhaps this was the way things were meant to be.

Maggie spoke, but I couldn't hear her over the thoughts reverberating in my mind.

It was time to let go. Of the past, of the might-have-beens, and of the guilt. And it was time to accept whatever God had in store for my future.

The thoughts pierced through me. It was time to choose. Hold on, or let go. I closed my eyes and felt myself release my grip on the past. A feeling of both weakness and relief flowed through me. *David, wherever you are, I hope and pray that you're happy. I wish you the very best.*

It seemed like a ridiculous time to make a major life decision, while waiting in terror to get Greta back, but perhaps it was really the perfect time. Everything seemed so clear.

I hear a slight rustle and turned to look at Maggie. She had pulled the paper out of her coat pocket and ran her fingers along it.

I checked my watch. We had another ten minutes or so before the meeting. I shifted from foot to foot, trying to keep warm. In the silence I walked from the center of the road to the side of the bridge. While the vehicle level was covered, it had large open arches in the brick, like windows. I moved and looked over the edge. Beneath us was a fast flowing river. I couldn't make out much in the darkness, but the sound of the rushing water was clear. It sounded like it was a long way down.

I heard Maggie approach behind me. "It's almost time, isn't it?"

I checked my watch again. "Almost. We should be ready for anything."

Chapter 45

A SET OF HEADLIGHTS at the far end of the bridge made my heart thump wildly. Wind whipped at us from the open sides of the bridge. This was it. There could be no mistakes.

I turned to Maggie and gave her hand a quick squeeze. She tightened her hand on mine, her grip almost painful, but I didn't draw away. I felt the waves of terror pumping off her like heat from the sun. I prayed as we stood like that.

God, protect Greta. Please, let us get her back, and help us to keep from putting more lives in danger tonight. You know how tonight is going to end. I pray that I would be able to trust that You are in control. Please Lord, help me to know what to do.

As the lights approached, the sound of tires

scrunching over snow got louder. Neither Maggie nor I moved from the center of the road where we stood, despite the fact that the car had yet to slow down. We held our ground and let the car screech to a stop, twenty feet in front of us.

My breath whooshed out, but I kept my shoulders squared and got my mind ready for battle.

The doors of the car flew open and out stepped two men. Both were dressed in long leather coats that reminded me of Soviet officer dress, but there wasn't a patch or insignia to be found on them anywhere. The lack didn't confuse my understanding of who they really were.

The man from the driver's side confirmed my thoughts when he spoke. "You have papers?" His Russian accent was unmistakable.

From the corner of my eye I saw Maggie hold out the rolled document.

"Where's the girl?" I demanded, my voice clear and strong.

The speaker shook his head. "Papers first."

I heard Maggie reach into her pocket, and I turned to see what she had. In one hand she held the paper and in the other she held a lighter. I heard the click and the hiss, a flame spat from it, and I could see from Maggie's face that she wasn't bluffing. "Greta. First."

The man turned, made some sort of hand signal, and immediately the rear door of the car swung open to reveal another man, this one with a rock solid grip around Greta's upper arm.

I had to look away for a second, keep my eyes off the child, so that I could keep my focus. I turned and saw Maggie doing the same. Neither of us would be able to follow through with the plan if we let our concentration waver.

"Bring her toward us. When I have her, I'll hand over the papers."

The big Russian shook his head. "Papers first."

I saw Greta twist and wriggle in the man's grip and broke into a grin when she kicked him as hard as she could in the shin. The Russian grunted and hunched forward a bit, but didn't let go. I looked at her face for the first time and saw that she didn't look in the least scared. She looked mad and a little dangerous. At least if I were in kicking range I might take a step back. I wanted to pull the feisty child into my arms for a well-deserved hug but settled for a grin instead.

"This is not a negotiation. I will have Greta in my arms before I hand over the paper." I heard the lighter click on again and wondered if they'd call her on her bravado. If they hurt Greta in any way Maggie would buckle.

There was a grunt, and the man who held Greta moved forward, crossing the span of distance between us, the little girl in tow.

Maggie trembled slightly, and I reached my hand out to steady her. I gave her arm a quick squeeze, then took the paper and lighter from her so she could move forward to meet Greta.

I watched as she shot across the last few feet, fell to her knees on the cement, and wrapped her arms around her child.

I took a step forward and handed the paper to the soldier in front of me. I felt a sick twist in my gut doing it. For all I knew I could be signing the death warrants of the men listed on that document. But there'd been no way to exchange it for a falsified document because of the official seal on this one. And so we had to trust that Jack would be able to fulfill his part of the plan. The lives of the men on that list depended on it.

I forced myself to let go of it, instead of crushing it in my fist.

I watched as the two Soviets by the car pulled out their guns and trained them on the three of us as they covered their man crossing the distance back toward the vehicle. He jumped into the backseat, slammed his door, and the front two did the same thing. With a screech of tires the car was flung into reverse and a pivot turn. Within seconds, the car was facing away from us and tearing back toward the Soviet sector.

As soon as they were no longer watching I grabbed Maggie's hand. "Run. Now."

She lifted Greta up off her feet, held her close, and we ran. We had to get off the bridge and out of sight.

Chapter 46

WE CLEARED THE bridge and just had time to duck behind the abutment before we heard it. A sharp echoing boom from inside the bridge tunnel, and another almost immediately after.

I knew it would be the explosion of the car tires from Jack's spike strip. When he'd told me his idea I'd been skeptical, but when he'd explained that a thin strip of wood studded with hundreds of nails could immobilize a vehicle I'd decided to trust him that it would work. As we'd been making the exchange Jack had laid it somewhere between there and the mouth of the bridge. I'd had to block the thought completely from my mind as the exchange was made, to keep myself from looking for him.

He now had the soldiers stopped, but the rest of his plan, three trained and armed soldiers against one ex-FBI agent, was terrifying to contemplate. But we couldn't let them have that document.

I tried to fight the urge to go back to help him. He'd told us to meet him in a hidden stairwell a few blocks away, but now that I knew Greta and Maggie were safe no power under heaven could keep me from going to help him.

I turned to Maggie, pulled Greta toward me, and gave her a giant hug. "You were as brave as a bear, little one." Greta grinned like she'd just spent the afternoon on some great adventure, and I couldn't help but smile.

"Okay, stay here. I'll be back as soon as I can."

Maggie nodded, apparently realizing that whether he knew it or not, Jack needed help.

Chapter 47

MAGGIE

MAGGIE RESISTED the urge to pace and settled instead for wrapping her arms around her daughter. Fear for Jack tore at her. She and Greta waited at the meeting point for more than an hour before they heard the sound of tires on the pavement. Holding out a hand to warn Greta to stay back, Maggie edged from between the shadows and watched as Allie slipped out of the driver's seat of a car. Her breath caught, but relief followed almost instantly as the passenger door opened to reveal Jack, safe and whole. Her relief was so strong it weakened her knees. He'd taken on the three Soviet soldiers, and he'd won. And he'd done it for her. Her and Greta.

Maggie picked up the child of her heart and carried her out from behind their hiding spot. There he was, big as life, a massive grin on his face when he saw them. He moved to the driver's seat, and Allie slipped into the back, letting Maggie and Greta into the front of the car. Maggie crossed the open space between the hiding spot and the car, feeling as though she were making a trench crawl with a thousand guns pointed at her. She slid in, but didn't breathe a sigh of relief until her door was closed and Greta was snuggled safely between her and Jack.

Only a split second after the door closed, Jack stomped on the accelerator and buzzed through the deserted street.

"What happened? Are you okay?" she asked, desperate to be sure.

"Fine," he said, never taking his eyes off the road. "But we don't have much time. We've got to get to the American base. It won't be long before someone on the Soviet side realizes those guys haven't come back and sends someone out to look for them."

"And where are they going to find them?" Allie asked.

"Let's just say that there is a lot more trunk room in their car than I would have believed."

Allie laughed, but Maggie still couldn't believe it had all worked. That in a matter of hours, this nightmare would be over.

"You got the document back?" She knew he wouldn't be here if he hadn't, but Maggie's mind wouldn't believe it until he said the words.

"I have the document." He paused. "But the new seal we put on it was broken."

Maggie felt her joy turn to ice at the words. "So one of them knows the names on that list."

Jack nodded. "And it's not going to be long before more of them do. The minute those officers get out of that trunk they're going to go back to the Soviet compound and see that the men on that list are rounded up and shot."

"So it was all for nothing then?" Maggie fought the intense desire to weep.

"Not for nothing. We have Greta back, and we have a few hours head start. I hope. We're going to have to find someone at the American base, and they will probably take it from there. I imagine they'll try to extract the men whose covers have been blown."

"But there's not really much chance. Is there?"

Jack shook his head. "We've done everything we can. The only other option would be to kill those three Russians, and that I won't do."

Maggie reached over the seat and laid her hand on Jack's shoulder.

"You are a good man Jack O'Connor."

Chapter 48

ALLIE

THE DRIVE TO the American base only took ten minutes, and as the city whizzed by outside my window I was profoundly thankful not to be walking. Trying to make it the ten miles or so from the bridge to the American headquarters would have been almost too much. I just wanted to sink into the seat of the car and sleep. Exhaustion—physical, mental, and emotional—seeped into every pore.

Jack had, through his new contacts on the base and his American passport, gotten permission to enter the American headquarters, and the guard posted at the perimeter waved us through when he recognized him.

Jack pulled into the compound and found his way to a parking lot of sorts, lined with covered trucks and military equipment. He threw the car into park and turned so he could see both Maggie and me.

"I ferried the kids from the orphanage here earlier."

"Where are they?" I asked.

"They're in one of the covered trucks over there. I gave two soldiers a few leftover bars of chocolate to watch them for me for a few hours. I imagine they're all asleep by now." He nodded in Greta's direction. "As is that one."

I leaned forward, and sure enough, Greta was fast asleep lying against Maggie's shoulder. She looked like she'd spent the day playing rather than being held hostage. I thanked God that He'd kept her protected.

"The convoy is slated to get moving around two a.m., so we have a while to sit and wait, but you might as well relax while I go and pass our information along."

Maggie nodded, apparently loathe to leave Greta's side. As tired as I was, I knew I wouldn't be able to sleep, and I shook my head. "I'll come with you. This is something I need to see through to the end."

Jack seemed to understand. We took care not to slam the car doors and waken Greta.

"Do you have any idea who we need to see?" I asked.

"I've got a name."

I looked around the sprawling camp. "And now if we only had a location."

Jack didn't slow. "That building." He pointed and kept walking.

I kept up, but just barely, with his determined stride. We got to the outside of the building and were momentarily stumped when we found the front doors locked. I leaned against the side of the building and tried to catch my breath.

"Have you actually looked at the document yet?" I asked.

He shook his head. "Other than to see that the seal was broken? No."

"Aren't you curious?" I asked.

"Curious?" His eyebrow went up.

"That's the wrong word. Don't you at least want to see the contents of the document that started this whole thing?"

He shook his head, but handed me the paper. Apparently I was the only one here who wanted to see what the fuss was all about. I tried to quash the desire, but couldn't, so I ran my fingers along the seam and unrolled it.

It was a numbered list. Three names. It was written in a cramped, hurried scrawl and it was hard to make out in the dimness of the camp. I moved closer to the dim overhead light of the Headquarters building and squinted at the paper.

The first name was Major Peter Koresec, the second was Captain Ivan Nikitin, and I really had to squint to read the last one.

The ground beneath me seemed to sway as I read the final name: Lieutenant Colonel David Rubeneski.

Chapter 49

THE DOCUMENT fell from my hand. I saw Jack look over at me, shake his head, and pick it up off the ground. He rolled it up without looking at it and shoved it back into his coat pocket.

"Sorry," I mumbled, barely able to breathe.

He nodded and looked away.

I tried to pull my thoughts together, but I felt like I was underwater, my brain cloudy.

Snippets of conversation came back to me. *"The minute they get out of that trunk, the men on that list are going to be rounded up and shot."*

My stomach heaved.

"It appeared to have been written by a spy within

the Allied military presence here. Whoever it was must have had a very high clearance level because he listed the names and ranks of three American moles within the Soviet military in Berlin."

David's name was on that list. David was an American spy in the Soviet military. And someone who knew what he was doing had betrayed him.

Distantly I felt my hands start to shake as understanding hammered down. He was going to be woken up, wherever he was, shoved outside, lined up against a wall, and shot. And that was the best scenario. The other scenarios, the ones where they wouldn't kill him immediately, were too terrifying to contemplate.

I looked up and saw that Jack was speaking to me. I could see his mouth moving, but my brain refused to register sound.

I tried to paste a neutral expression on my face, and I spoke loudly, to hear above the ringing in my ears. "Why don't I head back to check on Maggie and Greta while you're trying to find whoever you're trying to find." I laughed like something was funny, and Jack gave me a strange look, because there wasn't.

I forced myself to focus on the next few seconds. To be convincing. "Jack, I'm exhausted. I need to go sit down for a while."

"Oh. I'll walk you back."

"No." It came out too sharp, and slightly hysterical. I forced down the bubbling panic. "No.

There's not that much time left. You go do what you need to do, and I can easily find my way back to the car." I must have sounded closer to normal this time as the concerned look on his face faded.

"Okay, if you're sure."

I closed my eyes for a split second in sheer relief. I turned away from him and headed back in the direction we'd come as fast as I could without drawing attention.

Don't panic, don't panic, don't panic. I repeated the litany in my head, doing my best to stave off the terror that was within a hair's-breadth of swamping me.

Think, Allie. What is the next step? Make a plan.

Maggie, Jack, and all of the children were safe. They'd be on their way out of Germany within hours. They were going to be all right. Jack loved Maggie, Maggie loved Jack, everything was going to work out there.

I couldn't go with them. Obviously. They were going to have to leave without me. Jack wouldn't do it. He'd never leave without me. Not willingly. I knew this, it's why even in the midst of the shock of reading David's name on that deadly scrap of paper, I hadn't told him. He would stay with me; he would help me find David or die trying.

But Maggie needed him. Greta needed him. He needed to get them all out. They were counting on him. I was almost to the car and was no closer to a plan.

I was going to need the car. It was too far between here and the Soviet side to walk. I was going to have to either find a way to steal it or tell Maggie what was going on. I considered for a moment. Maggie would understand. I could tell Maggie. She could be the one to tell Jack—when it was too late to come after me.

I ran the last fifty feet to the car. I had to hold myself back from throwing the door open, with no regard to the sleeping child and possibly a sleeping Maggie.

I went to the passenger side and opened the door. I ducked in and saw Maggie raise her head. She'd either been sleeping or really close to it.

"Maggie, I'm sorry to wake you, but I really need to talk to you." I felt tears spring to my eyes. "Maggie, I need you."

She blinked her eyes, instantly awake. "Anything. What do you need?" she asked, knowing, realizing what total panic looked like.

"You remember when I told you that someday I'd tell you my story. About the man who haunted me?"

She nodded, her eyes wide.

"I don't have time to tell the story, but he's here. He's one of the men on your list." I couldn't find any more words. Saying it aloud made it even more real, and I felt the rise and crest of terror hit me again. I laughed, and it was a terrifying sound. Brittle and hysterical. "I haven't seen him in eight years. But that was his name on the list. David—"

"Rubeneski." She breathed. "I see those three names in my sleep."

"I've been looking for him since the end of the war. Just today I'd decided to let it go and move on with my life." I shook my head.

"What do you need, Allie? Anything."

"I don't know yet. I'll need the car for sure. I'm going to need you to keep Jack from finding out until it's too late." She shook her head, but I grabbed her hand and forced her to look at me. "You said 'anything,' Maggie. I need you to promise me. He can't know until I'm too far away to find."

She was quiet for a moment. "I owe you my life, Allie. Even more, I owe you Greta's life. I promise."

I breathed a sigh of relief. "I'll write him a note, but please, make him understand why I did it."

She nodded. I opened the glove compartment, found a scrap of paper and a pencil. I scribbled madly for several moments, then handed it to her along with my passport.

She shook her head when she saw it. "You can't give me that," she said.

"Take it. With all of the chaos tonight it might help you get out. And they're expecting Mr. Fortune and his wife to be taking these children out, so you're going to be Mrs. Fortune."

"What about you? You are going to need your passport if you want to get home. If you want to get your David out."

"I'll find another way. And nothing is going to stop me from getting us both back home," I promised.

"I believe you," she said. "You're an amazing woman, Allie Fortune."

I leaned forward and wrapped my arms around her. "So are you, Maggie O'Shayne. Take good care of Jack."

She smiled. "Thanks for bringing him back to me."

I smiled and fought back the tears. "Okay, I have to leave now. I'll see you back in New York soon," I promised.

She gathered Greta into her arms, and I got out, circled the car, and opened her door for her. I took a long look at both of them, memorizing their faces before suddenly remembering something. I fished in my coat pocket until I found my key ring. I pulled one off and handed it to Maggie. "This is for Jack. Tell him that there's room for an extra desk in my office, and I think there's just enough room for his name on the door, if he's interested."

Maggie took the key from me and nodded, then shoved the key into her pocket.

Chapter 50

I DIDN'T BREATHE easy until I was out of the compound. The sight of Maggie, Greta in her arms, waving to me, stayed in my mind as I drove away. Part of me was screaming, "What am I doing?" but a louder part of me was chanting, "Hurry, hurry, hurry."

I had no plan, no resources, and no allies.

I pulled over to the side of the road, leaned my head on the steering wheel, and tried to take deep breaths.

I had a few hours at the most to get into Soviet territory, find David, and get him out. The one thing I had going for me is that I knew vaguely where he was. All Soviet military personnel were stationed at the Soviet compound. Now I just had to find one particular soldier in a hive of enemies. I checked my watch. It was already one-thirty in the morning.

Okay, one thing at a time. I had to get onto the Soviet base. Maggie had said earlier today that it was on the other side of the bridge. Almost exactly at the end of the bridge. There was no way I could get onto the base by just driving across the bridge. But I did know of another way to get into that general area that was less conspicuous. A back way in.

I could get near the base. But how was I going to get on? And once I did get on, how was I going to find David?

Overwhelmed with the challenges, I wanted to surrender to the panic. I had no time to sit down and plan. The clock was ticking, and David's life was hanging in the balance.

Along a deserted street, I crossed the much smaller bridge and felt a warm lick of terror at the thought that I was now in Soviet territory. I shut off the headlights of the car and picked my way slowly along the street. Even in the dark it wasn't hard to see the perimeter of the Soviet compound. The roving light of a watchtower pretty much gave its identity away as a military installation. I pulled the car over to the side of the road, pocketed the keys, and forced myself out of the vehicle before I had a chance to talk myself out of it.

I knew next to nothing about Karlshorst, other than it had been the Soviet military headquarters since the end of the war. I didn't know what kind of security they had, how big it was, or how on earth I was going to find David once I actually got into the compound.

Saying a quick prayer for safety I crossed the road and walked up to the wire fence that surrounded the compound. A quick glance told me it was razor wire, stretched out tight, about five feet high. There was a dull gleam coming from the bits of sharpened metal, but I refused to let it intimidate me. I knew there were ways to cross razor wire, I just had to remember.

I stripped off my coat, felt the thickness of the felted wool, and knew that with it I'd be able to get over, mostly unscathed. Steeling myself I laid my coat on the highest rung of wire and started to climb.

Crossing to the inside of the compound I felt the scorching sting from what seemed like a thousand cuts, mostly centered on my legs and a few on my hands where the wire had punctured through the protective padding of my coat. Rivulets of blood slid down my calves, and I fervently hoped that there were no guard dogs on the premises. The scent of my blood would probably send them into a baying fury.

Looking around I tried to absorb the layout in front of me. The roving spotlight gave enough light for me to be able to see most of the compound. I couldn't see any guards from where I was, but that was no guarantee. I was in the treed perimeter and needed to head northeast toward the cluster of buildings. This was the most dangerous area, as there was little cover and there was the constantly moving spotlight. I leaned my back against a tree and tried to calm my breathing. Looking down I saw the hem of my skirt was torn to ragged shreds. I sighed at the bloody-looking mess, but an idea niggled at the back of my mind.

Pleased with the possibility I peered around the tree again and found the building closest to me. I would have to cross, in the open, the fifty feet between my tree and the building. I had a vague idea of the timing of the spotlight, but I sat and watched how it moved for several minutes before feeling confident that I could avoid it.

I sucked in a deep breath, checked the light, then ran, crouched, straight toward the smallish building. My shoes crunched on the snow, and my breathing sounded loud to my own ears. But apparently it wasn't loud enough to alert anyone of my presence in the stillness of the camp.

Leaning against the building, I tried to catch my breath. It heaved in and out in frozen clouds of vapor as I puffed. I peeked around the edge of the building to get a view of my surroundings from this perspective.

From here there were several buildings I could reach with just a quick sprint. I took a step back and looked at this one. It was relatively small, cement-colored with a brown door. Something was written in Russian above the door, probably what the building's purpose was, but it was of no help to me.

I tried turning the handle gently, but it wouldn't budge. Walking around to the side I checked the possibilities. About ten buildings were within my reach. Across a large open expanse was a massive building lined with windows that had to be either offices or barracks. I dashed to my left, to another building, this one bigger, and headed straight for the door. This one turned and I pushed the door open a crack.

The inside of the room was dark, but as I held my breath and listened, I could tell it was unoccupied. The air had the still feeling that meant it had lain undisturbed for a while. I slipped in, leaving the door slightly ajar behind me. Checking for the glint of windows in the darkness I didn't see any. I shoved my hand into my pocket, but didn't pull the flashlight out. Instead I turned it on while it was still in my coat, so there was only a slight glow through the heavy wool fabric. It wasn't much, not enough to attract any unwanted attention, but it was enough for me to assess that there were no windows in the building. Sighing with relief I shut the door behind me and pulled the flashlight out of my pocket.

In front of me was an open rectangular space, filled with supplies. *Yes!* I let out a quick grin and then turned to the racks of uniforms lining the wall. I picked and sorted through them for about five minutes before finding the smallest one in the middle of the rack. It would still be big, but not obviously so. I laid it aside and moved toward the boot wall. Hundreds of pairs of black army boots lined the wall, all hopelessly huge. Scanning the shelves, I finally found a pair that looked like they'd at least stay on my feet. A bin of woolen socks at my left provided the rest of the solution. I grabbed three pairs, to help keep the still-far-too-large boots on.

Delighted with my finds I crossed to another wall. Here were the heavy overcoats I'd seen on the soldiers around Berlin. I grabbed one and a rucksack that lay on the ground at my feet. It was full, and inside was a blanket, a pair of binoculars, and assorted other things. I didn't bother to empty it, just shut it, laid it with my appropriated things, and worked quickly to change myself into a Russian soldier. The clothes were thick and heavy, but I was fairly sure if no one looked too closely and if I was able to find a hat I'd pass for a young Russian soldier on a cursory glance. But truly, if anyone looked more closely than that, my rescue mission would already be over. I forced my thoughts away from the logical next step, what would happen to me if I was discovered.

Crumpling my clothes into a ball, I shoved them underneath two feet of socks in the bin. I covered the clothes up and tried to make it look normal before a thought occurred to me and I dug everything out again. I went through each garment of clothing, each pocket and label, to make sure there would be no incriminating evidence with my name on it left in the clothes. I already knew I'd have to find another place to dispose of my hat as it came from a small millinery in New York that wouldn't be hard to trace. I shoved it into the backpack, hefted the heavy green bag onto my shoulder, and looked for the last thing I needed for my costume. A bucket full of winter hats was exactly what I was looking for. The traditional leather and fur Russian hats with earflaps would cover most of my face if left down, and all of my hair even with the flaps up. I could probably pass for a baby-faced young soldier. In the dark. From a distance.

I hoped.

The cuts on my legs from the razor wire stung

as the rough material of the pants scraped at them, but overall, I was warmer and far less conspicuous than I'd been ten minutes ago.

I shut off the flashlight, tucked it into my pocket, and stepped out of the building.

Chapter 51

MAGGIE

MAGGIE WAS SITTING on the back edge of the truck where the children lay sleeping when Jack and another man approached. She saw him look around in confusion for the now missing car before spotting her. He adjusted his course toward her, the burly other man following along behind.

Fear rose up in her throat. She had Allie's passport, but anyone who took more than a moment to look at her would realize that she was the fugitive everyone in Berlin was looking for. Her hands started to shake. She was within a hair's-breadth of being discovered, and Jack was leading her downfall directly to her.

He crossed the last few steps to her and smiled. Everything in her was screaming to run, to hide, to get away, but the look on Jack's face couldn't have been clearer. It said, "Trust me." And as her panic abated, she realized that she already did.

"Margaret Katherine O'Shayne, meet Major General Henry Grey, the assistant deputy military governor here. In other words, the man in charge."

He'd used her name. Allie had given up her passport for nothing, and there was no way Maggie was going to get out of Berlin. Despair rose in her, but it was offset by the knowledge that Greta would still get out. That she would be safe. Maggie knew now that she would trust Jack with anything, even that which was most precious to her. Her daughter.

Maggie tried to keep the terrified-rabbit look out of her eyes, wanting to face whatever came with courage. She straightened her shoulders and raised her eyes to meet the man Jack had brought to her.

"It's good to meet you, Major General Grey." Her voice hardly trembled at the words.

"And it's about time I finally met you, Miss O'Shayne. You've caused quite a stir in this city over the past few weeks."

"And here I've been trying to lie low."

The major general laughed at that. "Too low. We've been scouring the streets to find you, with nary a reported sign, and then I find that you've walked right onto my base, pretty as you please."

Maggie shifted her eyes to Jack, trying to see what he expected her to say, but Jack just kept his eyes trained on the other man.

"I'm very sorry to say that I'm going to need you to answer some questions for me. And as much as I don't want to, I'm going to have to handcuff you first."

Nausea hit Maggie, churning her gut, but she simply nodded. The major general motioned with his hands, and immediately two uniformed soldiers appeared from either side of her. They moved to her sides, squeezing her between them, as their commanding officer rounded and cuffed her arms behind her back. All the while she kept her eyes on Jack. "Keep Greta safe," she mouthed. For a second she felt doubt creep in. Why had Jack turned her in? How was this keeping her safe? But almost as soon as the thoughts hit, she shoved them away. In the deepest part of her she trusted him to do the right thing.

The men on her side were gentle as they helped her cross to a building with several lighted windows. They traveled in silence, and she could hear the crunch of snow beneath her boots. She was escorted into the building, down a set of stairs, and into an office. No one broke the silence as they walked. She was helped into a chair, then the two guards left, leaving just her, the major general, and Jack in the room.

"I suppose you know why we've brought you here," the officer said.

"Because you believe that I killed two of your men in the market several weeks ago."

He rubbed his hand along his clean-shaven chin. "Actually, we already know you weren't the shooter. Figured that out a few days after the wanted poster of you came out."

Maggie drew in a sharp breath. "You know?"

"Don't look so surprised. We don't shoot the accused first and look for evidence later. We talked to witnesses, and we used the clues from the scene to help tell us what really happened. We know that both of our men died trying to protect you and what your little girl discovered."

She tried to ignore the flush of icy terror that skidded down her spine at the casual mention of Greta; instead she asked the only question she could think of. "Then why am I here in handcuffs?"

"Procedure mostly. You were an official suspect who went underground when we tried to find and question you; you had top-secret, vital information in your possession that endangered the lives of several of our people. I just wanted to make sure that I was actually going to get to talk to you, that you wouldn't run off before I'd had the chance to tell you that you've been cleared of all charges. And I wanted to tell you that the American army would be happy to escort you out of Berlin tonight. Assuming you want to go, that is."

Maggie tried to take it all in, but it was too much. Instead she blurted out another burning question. "What about those men? The Soviets must know their names by now. What are you going to do about them?"

The officer pinched the bridge of his nose for a second, then answered. "We've got a plan in place, and hopefully those men will be out of danger soon." He paused. "I must say though, if you and Agent O'Connor here hadn't brought this list to us when you did, there would have been no hope for these men. They have a fighting chance now because of your actions."

"So am I free to go?" She wanted no more beating around the bush, just a clear answer to a simple question.

"Yes, ma'am. You are free to leave now." He moved around and unlocked the cuffs from her wrists.

She pulled her hands forward and rubbed at the reddened spots where the metal had pinched.

"Then if I'm free to go, I'd like to get back to my child now. All of the children actually."

"That's a good idea, ma'am. The convoy is waiting for both of you."

Maggie just shook her head at the reversal of circumstances in the past few hours. Jack stopped, whispered something to the major general, and then threaded his fingers through hers as he led her out of the office.

Maggie kept silent as they crossed the base back to the trucks, mentally replaying the last half hour over again in her mind until something the major general said finally registered.

"He called you Agent O'Connor."

Jack turned to her and grinned. "He did. Once I knew what the document contained, I knew I had to inform the Americans. I came over, got an emergency meeting with the commanding officer of the base, and laid all of my cards on the table. Including the fact that I was a federal agent back home. They made a few calls, verified that I was who I said I was, and I set up a time to bring you in."

"So you've had a plan all along?"

"If by 'all along' you mean the last four hours, yes. I've had a plan all along."

Maggie couldn't restrain herself. She smacked him on the arm. "Next time, let me in on the plan."

Jack just grinned. "Does that mean there's going to be a next time?"

Maggie sighed. "I am not set up for this kind of thing. Maybe you and Allie thrive on adventure, but give me a plain and simple battlefield operating room any day." She regretted the words as soon as they left her mouth.

"Speaking of Allie, where's she gotten off to? I haven't seen her since we went to drop off the list."

Center Point Publishing
600 Brooks Road ● PO Box 1
Thorndike ME 04986-0001 USA

(207) 568-3717

US & Canada:
1 800 929-9108
www.centerpointlargeprint.com